PAYBACK IS FOREVER

NICK KOLAKOWSKI

ADVANCED PRAISE
PAYBACK IS FOREVER
BY NICK KOLAKOWSKI

"With **PAYBACK IS FOREVER**, Nick Kolakowski has crafted a quick, clever story that feels both classic and fresh. This one hits the ground running and never lets up. Highly recommend."
—**Steve Weddle**, author *Country Hardball*

"Like a demented fun-house mirror version of a Richard Stark novel, Kolakowski deconstructs hoary crime cliches with the sort of panache you don't want to miss. Our tour guide, Miller, is cut from the tough-guy mold, but twisted so askew by the end of the book, he's carved out his own niche."
—**Brian Asman**, author of *Man, F*ck This House*

More titles by Nick Kolakowski

(Shotgun Honey Books)

A Brutal Bunch of Heartbroken Saps
Slaugherhouse Blues
Main Bad Guy
Love & Bullets: Megabomb Edition

(Down & Out Books)

Boise Long Pig Club
Rattlesnake Rodeo
Maxine Unleashes Doomsday

(Other releases)

Absolute Unit
Lockdown:
Stories of Crime, Terror, and Hope During a Pandemic

*"His name is Miller...
He's a professional thief...
Surrounded by killers and freaks!"*

PAYBACK IS FOREVER
Nick Kolakowski

2022

PAYBACK IS FOREVER
Text copyright © 2022 Nick Kolakowski

All rights reserved. This book or any portion thereof may not be reproduced or used in any manner whatsoever without the express written permission of the publisher except for the use of brief quotations in a book review.
This book is a work of fiction. Names, characters, places, and incidents either are products of the author's imagination or are used fictitiously. Any resemblance to actual persons, living or dead, events, or locales is entirely coincidental.

Published by **Shotgun Honey Books**

215 Loma Road
Charleston, WV 25314
www.ShotgunHoney.com
Cover by Bad Fido.

First Printing 2022.

ISBN-10: 1-956957-05-7
ISBN-13: 978-1-956957-05-1

9 8 7 6 5 4 3 2 1

To Lucien—

Make of this what you will.

PAYBACK IS FOREVER

CHAPTER 1

WHILE THE SHOOTOUT PAUSED SO EVERYBODY COULD RELOAD, MILLER wondered whether the clown was still alive.

The clown had taken three shots to the chest and collapsed beside the Tilt-a-Whirl. Miller hated the idea of civilian deaths, but at least he could tell himself it was the security guard's fault. If the security guard had stayed on the floor of the money room like a good little boy and not decided to march after them like Wyatt Earp, the clown would have continued to spread good cheer to the crowds of kids and parents. If the security guard had stayed on the floor, Miller's partners might have waited to spring the ambush he expected all along.

But the security guard had decided his employer's profits were worth dying for, and so Miller found himself crouching behind a dumpster as the uniformed idiot knelt to shoot at him from twenty feet away. Bullets smacked the dumpster's side with gonglike booms. From the Whack-a-Mole booth to his left, Bernard and Trent—up until two minutes ago, his partners in this little entrepreneurial endeavor—did their best to fill him and the security guard with lead. The clown lay in the crossfire, his oversized feet twitching.

If he made it out of this alive, Miller vowed to never rob an amusement park again.

When the firing stopped, Miller reloaded his .45 automatic. Bernard had a 9mm, which would have been worrisome if he could aim, but Trent's pump-action shotgun was the real problem. The shotgun would put Miller down if he broke into the open at the wrong moment. While Miller could use the screaming crowd as cover, he preferred if a family wasn't gunned down on his account.

Sirens in the distance meant Miller needed to end this soon. He knelt and stuck his gun under the dumpster, sighted on a khaki-clad leg, and pulled the trigger twice. The guard's knee shattered and he fell onto his face. If this had been France, Miller would have followed that up with a shot to the top of the kid's head, but he was no longer a soldier.

Hoisting the duffel bag full of cash onto his shoulder, Miller sprinted down the concourse, dodging left to put the Ring Toss O' Rama between him and any incoming bullets. Bernard fired anyway, the round cracking into wood. Trent's shotgun boomed, hitting nothing.

They expected him to head for the black sedan parked in the back lot, the same one they'd driven here, but Miller had other ideas. He ducked left again, down the concourse with kiddie rides on either side, firing twice in the air to clear the panicking civilians, hoping none of them would decide to play hero by leaping at him. He angled for the outer fence where he cut a hole a few days ago, and the green Buick parked in the weeds beyond. He was going to get away clean—but damn if he wouldn't feel bad about that clown.

CHAPTER 2

AS HIDING PLACES WENT, YOU COULD DO WORSE THAN THE VILLAGE ON A rainy Tuesday night.

The bartenders at McSorley's Old Ale House, on East 7th Street, liked to point to the dusty wooden chair tied to the ceiling and claim Abraham Lincoln had sat his bony ass in it a hundred years ago. It was just one of three-dozen historical souvenirs bolted, nailed, or roped to the bar's time-darkened surfaces, including ten dusty wishbones on a string above the bar, left behind by boys bound for France in World War I.

Miller cared nothing about history. He just wanted McSorley's fine ale in his stomach. It was a small reward for a messy victory. The take from the amusement park had come to five thousand dollars in small bills, a solid haul until he added up his expenses. Five hundred to Jonsey, the aging safecracker who sniffed out the score. Another fifteen hundred combined to the gun guy and the wheels guy. The remaining money, stashed under the floorboards of his apartment, would last for five months. Maybe longer if he kept his worst habits in check.

He had a lot to drink about. According to the newspapers, the clown had died instantly. Miller saluted the air with his beer glass. It's a hard world for the little guys, especially those who wear a red nose to make a living.

Soon it was seven, one of McSorley's quieter hours. The businessmen had cleared out after a beer or four, headed for the trains that would take them back to the suburban houses they quietly despised. It would be another hour or two before the first hipsters and poets and pin-jabbers and dodos, the folks who gave the Village its special flavor, drifted through the doors. From his chosen table against the bar's rear wall, Miller watched the professional drinkers clustered at the front tables, their heads wreathed in cigarette smoke. At the bar, a lone man stood with his back to Miller, peering out the rain-speckled windows at the colorful smears of passing cars.

Something aside from the dead clown was bothering him. After a bad job, he never had more than three beers. Hell, rarely more than two. Yet here he was, five pints in, which he took as a signal his mind was trying to slow down and work something out. But what?

Was he worried about his former partners? No. The newspapers, after mentioning the tragic obliteration of the guard's kneecap and the clown's head, had breathlessly described Bernard and Trent shooting their way through a police roadblock and escaping. But neither of them knew Miller's real name or where he spent his time.

No, his mind kept returning to gloves. Black leather gloves, so thin he could pick up a dime while wearing them. The kind he preferred on a job like the amusement park. He was diligent about slipping on the gloves hours before a score went down, and not removing them until after the escape. It wasn't the kind of detail he would overlook.

Except now, as he relived those frantic five minutes in the money room, he wondered whether his gloves had stayed on. He took pride in keeping everyone as calm as possible during a robbery, but Bernard and Trent had screamed and waved their weapons like amateurs, distracting Miller at a crucial moment. The lid on one of the money drawers had stuck, the key kept slipping from his grasp, and so he had…

Damnit!

…stripped off his left glove. Just for a second, so he could open the drawer. Had he wiped the metal down after clearing out the cash and putting the glove back on?

He had no memory of doing so.

Miller had only done one brief stint on a prison farm in Texas, on a trumped-up weapons charge, but that was enough to put his fingerprints in a file with his real name on it. Although he had changed identities five times in the nine years since that stint, he was in deep trouble if the cops ran any fingerprints from the money room against their files.

They would try to pin the death of that clown on him.

One of the bartenders wandered over. "Want another, brother?"

No McSorley's ale in prison, Miller thought. "Sure."

"On the house." The bartender wore a white jacket with long sleeves, which contrasted with his deeply tanned and lined face. A pink scar ran up the left side of his neck. "Listen, the one fancy-pants fellow standing at the bar…"

"Yeah?"

"He keeps asking about you. Actually, it's his damn doll keeps asking about you."

"What?"

"He's got a ventriloquist's doll with him. Makes it talk every time he orders another beer, too. And he keeps ordering beers, otherwise I'd have kicked him out a long time ago. I already got poets in here shouting about Moloch and Carl Solomon, getting gowed up in the shitter." The bartender stepped aside so Miller could have a better look at the man, who had shifted so he faced the bar instead of the window. Beside the man's half-empty beer glass sat the doll, dressed in a tuxedo, its glass eyes reflecting the bar's yellowish light.

"Maybe his doll thinks I'm handsome," Miller said.

"I thought you should know. Be back with that beer."

Miller nodded his thanks. Under ordinary circumstances, he was good at sensing when someone was observing him. Yet he had been so preoccupied with the possibility of fingerprints he had missed a stranger glancing his way in an almost-empty bar. A stranger armed with a ventriloquist's doll.

Who knew what terrible things someone with a ventriloquist's doll was capable of?

The bartender retreated behind the bar to fill a new glass, and the man with the doll turned to face Miller. He had a round face and an expensive haircut that was growing unruly at the edges. He wore a white dress shirt with the sleeves rolled up, and a pair of black suit pants too tight for his legs.

When the man met Miller's gaze, he picked up the doll in one hand and his beer in the other. Miller slipped a hand into his coat pocket and cupped the .25 pistol he kept there.

The man stopped a few feet from Miller's table, the doll cradled in his left arm.

"I don't know you," Miller said.

"No, you don't," the man replied, in a jocular voice that reminded Miller of a radio host.

The dummy in his arms opened its wooden jaws and rasped, in an accent fit for the Queen's tea table, "But buddy, do I know you."

"Best if you leave, Jeeves." Miller told the doll, before

shifting his gaze to the man. "And take Bertie Wooster here with you."

"Ah, a man who reads," the doll responded.

"I'll chop you into firewood," Miller said.

The pasty man jutted his chin at Miller's pocketed hand. "I'd love to take something out to show you. I'll do it slowly, so you don't decide to ventilate me with whatever cannon you got tucked in there."

"Fine."

With a theatrical sigh, the man placed the doll on the sawdust-coated floor. Reaching into his tight pants, he extracted something small and placed it on the table in front of Miller. It was a bullet with a dimple in the primer, from a misfire.

"From my employer, Mister Redfield," the man said, enunciating 'Mister Redfield' with a hammy glee. "It's very valuable to him, for reasons I'm sure you remember. He'd like to see you."

Miller picked up the bullet and rolled it between his fingers, studying the dimple. Memories of a sweaty night in New Orleans, the dark thrumming with insects, the smell of blood salty in the air. "What if I say no?"

Draining his beer, the man slammed his empty glass on Miller's table before bending to retrieve the doll. "You won't," he said, slipping a hand into the doll's back and standing again. "He informed me that you always pay a debt."

"Yeah? This is the payback?"

"Yes. He says he needs protection."

The doll spoke in thickest cockney: "Protection from dangerous men."

CHAPTER 3

"MY NAME IS SCOTT," THE MAN SAID, ONCE MILLER PAID AND THEY EXITED McSorley's into the dripping night. "I've been with Mister Redfield for two years. More than a friend, less than a wife, know what I mean? And this," meaning the doll, "is my best friend in the whole wide world, Colonel Longshanks."

"Wonderful," Miller said, both hands in his pockets, his finger resting lightly on the trigger of the .25. The street was empty but that meant nothing. If someone wanted to kill him, they could wait in a parked car until he walked past, then shoot him in the back. He was a meticulous man who prided himself on his stealth, but it was clear he had patterns to reconsider. If a doll-brandishing chump like Scott could find him, what would prevent Bernard and Trent from doing so? Or the cops, for that matter?

You're slipping, whispered a voice in his head. It sounded like his old drill sergeant, a grizzled slab of beef who liked to bend close and hiss through clenched teeth how you were going to die with a German bayonet rammed up your tradesman's entrance unless you learned how to reload faster.

"Where are we going?" Miller asked, rooted beside the bar's front door.

"You're a real Hard Harry, aren't you?" Scott said. "Mister

Redfield is in a house off Union Square. We're going there, if that's okay with you?"

"We're off to see the Lord in his manor," Colonel Longshanks purred, his tone lecherous.

"Mister Redfield? You ever just call him Rick?" It took a heroic effort on Miller's part not to rip off the doll's head and punt it into the street. "Why didn't he come himself?"

"Don't you worry your pretty little noggin," Colonel Longshanks purred, "for the Lord shall explain everything."

Miller grunted. "He'll explain how I shoved you up someone's ass?"

Scott frowned. "Don't insult the Colonel. He's got more military experience than you or me combined."

"Unless the 'Colonel' spent fifteen months slogging across France and Germany, I doubt that. How did you find me?"

The frown flipped into a grin. "He said you always go to McSorley's when you're in the Village, and you're usually in the Village after you've just pulled a job. Then he showed me a newspaper clipping about an amusement park robbery."

Too easy, Miller thought. As much as it hurts, you might have to give up McSorley's for good. "I don't know anything about a robbery," he said.

"Sure, whatever you say. You were probably tutoring nuns when the crime took place. Can we go? I didn't bring an umbrella, this shirt's expensive, and the Colonel doesn't like getting wet."

"God forbid," Miller said.

As they headed north through the moist night, Miller made a point to position himself between Scott and the street. There was almost no chance someone would take a shot at him, yet deep in his skull, his drill sergeant rasped on a murderous loop: *you're slipping, you're slipping…*

Rick's home off Union Square was a miniature castle

of dark stone squeezed between two apartment buildings. Its turret even had a battlement at the top. The front doors were blocked by an ornamental iron gate. Scott unlocked the gate and the door behind it before waving for Miller to follow him inside.

The castle's foyer could have belonged in an English manor. Mounted heads of elk and deer and moose lined the paneled walls, along with gold-framed oil paintings large enough to block the entrance to the Holland Tunnel. It smelled of wood polish and old money.

Locking the gate and door behind them, Scott nodded down the front hallway. "Living room, down and to the left."

"You lead off," Miller gripped Scott's elbow and squeezed, hard. "I'm in no mood."

"If that's your pleasure," Colonel Longshanks said, as Scott winced in pain.

As they marched down the hallway, Miller regretted the excessive number of beers downed this evening. The alcohol slackened his reflexes. They passed through a tall archway, entering a living room fit for a medieval king. Heat pulsed from a roaring fireplace set into the longest wall. Firelight glimmered off row upon row of leather-bound books on the floor-to-ceiling shelves.

Miller's feet sank to the ankles in a thick rug patterned with vines and lions. In the middle of the room, in one of four leather chairs arranged around a gold-lined table, sat Mister Redfield—Rick, to his friends. A thick cigar smoldered in Rick's left hand, a full glass of red wine in his right. He was a stocky fellow with short, thinning hair and long, graying sideburns.

When Rick saw Miller, his face popped with joy and he rose on shaky knees, the cigar waving like a drunk orchestra leader's baton. "My God, man," he said. "How long's it been?"

"Four years." Miller stopped in the middle of the room, angling himself by habit to keep both Rick and Scott in his field of vision. Four years ago, Rick lived in a fourth-floor studio on the border of Harlem, dreaming of a crazy scheme that would make him wealthy. Importing wood from Brazil, if Miller remembered correctly. Had that plan, despite all odds, actually succeeded? How else would Rick have landed a castle like this?

"It's been so long." Rick shook his head in wonder. "Yet it seems like yesterday."

"Does it?" Miller said.

Rick gestured to the table, topped with a tray loaded with bottles. "Drink? Whiskey, right?"

"That's right."

"Good man." Stuffing the cigar into the corner of his mouth, Rick stumbled to the tray and poured a glass of whiskey almost to the brim. "I know you love your harder stuff. McSorley's doesn't serve anything other than beer, though, right? Which makes me wonder why you always choose that place."

"It's quiet." Miller took the offered drink. "There's no bullshit. Except when guys show up with their dolls."

Rick grinned at Scott. "I think he means you."

"I'll duel the bastard at twenty paces!" Colonel Longshanks, cradled in Scott's arms, snapped back. Scott was so good at ventriloquism that his cheeks barely twitched as the doll spoke.

"What do you want, Ricky?" Miller asked.

Ricky squinted, swaying on his feet. "All business, huh?"

"I just got done a job. I'm not in a business mood."

"You will be in a few moments," Rick said. "I've entered into an arrangement with some… men of violence, shall we say. Which means I need the services of the most violent man I know. Which is you."

"I'm no bodyguard."

"No. You're capable of terrible acts, and that's the necessary thing here. Besides, bodyguards ask too many questions." Ricky rolled his eyes. "They're all former cops. Blab everything to their former colleagues when they're all drunk together. Can't have that, can we?"

"Who are your partners in this arrangement?"

Rick waved off the question. "No need for names. It's a simple handoff. Your salary is ten thousand dollars once the transaction is complete. Fair?"

Rick tried to keep his poker face intact. "That's a lot of money."

"Ah, you've always been a master of understatement. It's a fortune for one day's work—hell, for a year. Let's say the payment is for old times' sake. I could ask you to do it for free, because you owe me, but I believe in a fair wage."

Miller sipped his whiskey, letting the moment build. He would do it, of course, because it was a lot of money. "What day is this taking place?"

"Wednesday midnight."

Two nights from now. "Fine. Where?"

"They haven't told me yet. Somewhere in the city."

"When are they giving you the details?"

"Telephoning tomorrow morning, they said."

Miller set his whiskey on the table and stepped back. "Then I'll be back tomorrow morning."

"You could spend the night here." Rick waved his cigar at the ceiling. "Lots of bedrooms in this townhouse. We got a bowling alley in the basement and a fantastic yard out back."

"No."

Rick frowned. "No interest in reminiscing with an old chum?"

"See you tomorrow." Halfway to the archway, Miller stopped. "Ricky? How'd you afford this house?"

Rick's frown deepened. "My dashing good looks, old chum. My dashing good looks."

CHAPTER 4

MILLER RETURNED TO HIS TINY APARTMENT ON AVENUE B. A MONK WOULD have found the space nicely minimalist. The mattress on the bedroom floor was the largest piece of furniture. His money, along with an assortment of weapons and tools, lay beneath the floorboards of the short hallway separating bedroom from bathroom.

On his way home from Rick's castle, Miller had stopped at an all-night burger place on Avenue A and ordered the Big Jumbo Delight, two patties slathered with cheese and horseradish mayonnaise. Swallowed it down in a back booth while watching the fluffs and glue-sniffers try to hustle the boy behind the register. It was a delicious meal but the greasy meat sat heavy in his stomach as he undertook his usual evening ritual.

After setting a suitcase against the front door, he retrieved a wineglass from the small kitchen and filled it with small, tinkling bells. He set the glass atop the suitcase, positioning it carefully so it would tip forward if someone opened the door.

With his intruder alarm rigged, he undressed and lay in bed. Far below, on the street, a guitar thrummed the humid air, punctuated by the metallic rattle of a tambourine. A singer erupted in a fierce caterwaul that settled into rapid-fire lyrics, more spoken than sung, about nuclear fire and the angels.

Miller sighed. Yet another band of hipsters refusing to die with the song still inside them. He applauded the effort, but why did they always choose his street corner for these late-night jam sessions? Taking a deep breath and holding it, he focused inward, down and down and down, until the slow thrashing of his heart drowned out the music.

If Rick is willing to pay someone like me ten thousand dollars, he thought as he stared at the ceiling, it means the deal is already falling apart somehow. Ten thousand dollars promises pain and death. No sense in worrying about it now, though. Not until you learn more tomorrow.

Lulled by his heartbeat, the music reduced to a dim tone, he drifted toward oblivion—when a new noise broke through, soft but arrhythmic enough to snap him fully awake.

Creak.

Oh, you bastard.

Creak. Creak. Creak.

The old man upstairs knew he was home.

Creak-creak-creak-creak.

It sounded like the rocking chair was positioned directly overhead. You ancient limp-dicked wrinkly bastard, Miller wanted to yell. You waited until you heard my front door click, and then you waited another twenty minutes until you figured I was in bed, and then you started riding that rocking chair like a rodeo cowboy.

Creakcreakcreakcreakcreakcreak—

Miller was tempted to pry open a floorboard, retrieve one of his pistols, and fire a round into the ceiling. To warn the old man, not to kill him. But a shot might bring cops, even in this part of town. Instead, he rolled onto his side and placed the thin pillow over his ear, trying hard to plunge into sleep as he wondered why the hell this old bastard wanted to torture him.

CHAPTER 5

THE MORNING NEWSPAPERS OFFERED PRECIOUS FEW DEVELOPMENTS about the amusement park massacre. The police had discovered the robbers' vehicle at a rest stop, abandoned and burned. The police said they had leads on the suspects. They were probably lying.

I've spent fifteen years in this peculiar profession, Miller mused as he sipped his coffee at the little shop across the street from his apartment. Never had one screw up quite this badly. At least I got all the money.

Once Miller finished his coffee, he walked south. He was dressed in jeans and an N-1 deck jacket a little too warm for the weather. He blended in with the workmen swarming toward the docks. His heart leapt as it always did when he spied the Williamsburg Bridge. His grandfather had helped erect that enormous finger of steel and concrete arching its way across the East River.

He paused outside a Chinese restaurant, knelt, and rapped three times on the rusty sheet-doors covering the cellar stairs. The thud of a lock sliding back, and one of the doors lifted an inch, revealing a reddened eye squinting in the morning light. The eye found Miller and widened. The door slammed down again.

Miller waited, his right hand resting on the .25 in his

jacket pocket. Last night's rain had cleaned the air and sidewalks. From inside the restaurant came the smell of fresh oil boiling, which made his stomach growl. Maybe after this unpleasant business was over, he could stop inside the restaurant for dumplings and rice. Sometimes he enjoyed a second breakfast.

The cellar doors opened again, revealing a hulking man with a dry red beard. His eyebrows rising, he said, "You come bearing gifts?"

Miller tapped his jacket pocket. "Indeed. Always good to see you, Jonsey."

"You say that now." Jonsey disappeared down the stone stairs, leaving Miller to follow him after closing and locking the cellar door. They navigated past a storeroom into a narrow brick hallway, arriving at a rusted iron door. Jonsey unlocked the door with an ornate key.

They entered a room that looked like a combination of shooting range and church. On the far side, shredded paper targets hung on a brick wall scarred by bullet impacts. The near side was a jumble of workbenches, battered metal lockers, and tools, eyed coolly by a line of marble saints on a shelf. They seemed to disapprove of the partially disassembled pistols on the central workbench.

"Grab a seat," Jonsey said, after locking the door behind them. "Oops, wait, there's no place to sit. It's a real crazy alley down here."

"Your hospitality knows no equal." Miller leaned against the wall.

"I read the papers. Looks like you had a real mess down there. Those boys tried to cop a heel."

"I made it out."

"Yeah, you did. That was lucky. Maybe next time you're not so lucky."

"I'd never talk. Nobody's gonna put a cross on me."

"I hope not. But no offense, kid, I'm upright and breathing after all these years because I don't take what anyone tells me at face value. I know a nose when I smell one."

"How's this for face value?" Miller took the fat envelope from his pocket and placed it on the nearest locker.

"How much in there?"

"Your usual, plus five hundred. Call it a retainer, you hear of anything good. No more amusement parks."

"I might have something for you. Armored car score, Jersey. Easy play, take them on the highway."

"Who's the finger?"

"Dispatcher. Wants ten percent. The take might be fifty grand."

"This dispatcher, what's his story?"

"Used to be a cop."

Miller shook his head. "No. Can't trust a former cop as a finger. They always have an angle."

"This guy, he's no slim, but okay, forget about it. Something juicy comes up, you're my first call." Retrieving a pistol from the central workbench, Jonsey fiddled with the empty cylinder. "Listen, something else I gotta tell you, and no way in hell do I want to be in the middle of this, okay?"

"Okay."

"Trent called me last night. From a payphone in Pittsburgh. At least, that's where he said he was calling from. He was asking if you were alive."

"How considerate of him."

"I said I had no idea, that I didn't care. He kept calling you 'Victor,' so I assume you never slipped up and told him your real name."

"No, I'm always good about that."

"You tell him where you live? Any details?"

"Of course not. He knows I'm out of New York," Miller shrugged. "But it's a big city."

"Given how angry he sounded, I bet he's coming here with his buddy. Give them another day or two to dodge the roadblocks, plus a day to drive here. If you got someplace else to go that's not the city, I'd go there. Just for a little while."

"You don't think the cops will get them?"

"Newspaper said a clown got killed, plus an employee. Anyone else?"

Miller shook his head. "I shot a guard in the kneecap. Didn't kill him, though."

"You're getting soft in your old age. If you didn't kill one of their own, cops are less interested in your scalp. Trent and his buddy, I bet they'll go west, loop up through Ohio, come back. That's what I'd do, at least. Yeah, call it three days and they're here."

Miller considered Trent, bony and tall with a nose shaped like a meat cleaver. An ex-con who seemed dull until you talked money, a topic that made his eyes gleam with animal cunning. A Pittsburgh boy, or so he said. Trent had come recommended as someone who knew the logging roads they planned to use to escape the amusement park. For that reason alone, Miller had signed him on.

Then you had Bernard, who sat quietly until someone mentioned politics, at which point he would talk and talk and talk about how much he hated that prick John F. Kennedy. Bernard thought Kennedy was a pretty boy without his father's massive bootlegging balls. While Bernard lacked Trent's viciousness, he was just as dangerous with a gun.

"They always planned to cross me," Miller said. He had known it long before the amusement park, because guys like Trent and Bernard always crossed you. You might as well expect a crow to never fly.

"Remember what I told you? Don't get into bed with them. If you didn't gamble so much, you wouldn't get jammed up like this." Jonsey broke the pistol into three pieces. "Anything else I can help you with? Or you stop by just to hear my melodious voice?"

"I need a new gat."

"Don't you have a gun guy?" Jonsey set the pistol parts on the workbench.

"You sell guns, right?"

"Well, I'm not your usual gun guy. You buy a gun from me, it's at a premium, okay? Hundred-twenty. Because it's a gun meant for someone else."

"I'm not limited." Reaching into his pocket, Miller pulled out his roll and peeled off the requested amount in twenties. "I don't need anything fancy. Just something with power."

"You need to stop carrying around that dinky excuse for a firearm, that .25." Jonsey bent to the large safe beside the workbench, wincing as his knees cracked under his weight. "That shit couldn't stop a mouse."

"It's small. Good walking-around gun."

"If you say so." The safe shuddered open, and Jonsey pulled out a pistol wrapped in a white cloth. "This here's a .38 Smith & Wesson on a .44 frame. Use it in good health. And if you see Trent and his buddy, remember, shoot first."

Miller slipped the new pistol into the left pocket of his jacket. Carrying two weapons made him feel absurd, like a Western outlaw. But at least he felt a little safer.

CHAPTER 6

MILLER STOPPED IN THE CHINESE RESTAURANT ABOVE JONSEY'S LAIR, where he ordered beef dumplings. He regretted not carrying a flask of whiskey, because Chinese food and a couple shots of high-proof was the breakfast of champions.

Before returning uptown, he stopped at a phone booth and dropped a dime. Dialed a familiar number.

A man's voice: "Hello?"

Damnit. He hung up. Rammed a foot against the side of the booth, as if that would accomplish anything. Retrieved his food from atop the phone and walked up the avenue at high speed. If she had a man over, it was her right.

Rick's townhouse seemed less impressive in the brutal light of morning. Miller paused beneath an overhang across the street, scorching his fingertips and tongue on the hot dumplings but not caring, lost in the deliciousness of boiling juices and meat. It would probably give him heartburn later, and would surely clog his arteries a bit more, but what did that matter if he had almost no chance of living to fifty, much less sixty? You could do whatever you wanted if you were willing to pay the bill at the end.

As he ate, he watched Rick's windows. He watched the windows of the adjoining apartment buildings. He watched the street and the people on it, their heads bowed and shoulders hunched against the fresh wind sweeping from the Hudson. Nobody else was watching Rick's house.

Dumplings finished, he licked his fingers, tossed the crumpled container into the nearest trashcan, and crossed the street, angling for Rick's front door. As he did, a car roared past, missing him by inches before taking a screeching right turn at the far intersection. On the sidewalk, he passed a small boy in a red cap and a blue jacket, no more than ten years old, bouncing a blood-colored ball on the sidewalk.

He knocked on the gate. Scott opened the door and said, "Good. Just in time for breakfast."

"You live here?" Miller asked.

"Sometimes, sure." Scott ran a hand through his tangled hair. The smudges under his eyes hinted at a sleepless night. "Come on in. Take off your shoes, though."

"What?"

Unlocking the gate, Scott jabbed a finger at Miller's boots. "Your shoes. Take them off."

Miller pushed past him into the foyer. "Why are you whispering?"

"Just do it, okay? Rules of the house, at least for this morning."

"No." Miller strode down the hallway, Scott on his heels. "Please?"

"No. Where's Rick?" There was nobody in the living room. Ducking through another doorway, Miller found himself in an enormous dining room bathed in soft light through gossamer curtains. Rick sat at the long table, the remains of a considerable breakfast on the plate in front of him, a napkin tucked into the collar of his blue dress shirt. Colonel Longshanks sat in the chair to his left, barely tall enough to peek over the edge of the table, an empty plate in front of him.

At the head of the table sat an impossibly ancient woman, her frail body wrapped in a loose silk robe, her white hair pinned back in a rough bun. Her eyes, sheathed with faint cataracts, stared into eternity.

"Why, hello," Rick said, startled.

"Hope I'm not interrupting," Miller said.

"No, no, we have plenty left. Come in." Standing, Rick gestured toward the silver trays in the center of the table, piled high with eggs and bacon and little curls of pink flesh Miller guessed was fish. Of more interest to Miller was the carafe of what smelled like coffee. Whiskey might have been part of the breakfast of champions, but coffee was the elixir of the gods.

"Good," Miller said. He moved toward the table, stopping when Ricky gestured at his feet.

"Shoes," Rick said, glancing at the old woman with fear.

"What about my shoes?"

"Take them off."

"I wore them in the house last night," Miller said, enjoying how such a simple statement made both Scott and Rick stiffen with terror.

The old woman remained frozen as a statue. Miller noted the chunky rings on her fingers. Enough gold there to buy a car. The necklace around her neck, its diamonds glittering in the light, was also worth a small fortune.

"Hello," Miller said to her, but the old woman offered no sign of recognition.

"That's Lady Hardy," Scott said, as if that somehow explained everything.

"She got a thing against shoes?" Miller asked.

"They ruin the carpets," Rick said, sitting again. "Wear down the weave."

"And this is her house," Miller said, pouring himself a full cup of coffee.

"Of course," Rick offered.

"Of course," Scott said, in a startlingly effective parody of Rick's voice.

"Don't you dare," Rick snapped at him.

"And she's okay with you here?" Miller asked.

"She's okay with it so long as folks take their shoes off," Scott said, again imitating Rick. The man's skill with voices was uncanny.

"I am warning you," Rick growled at him.

Miller chose to ignore their spat. "Lady Hardy," he said. "Do you object to me wearing my shoes in here?"

No reply from Lady Hardy.

"I think I'm in the clear." Sipping his coffee, Miller turned to Rick. "Your men of violence call yet?"

"No. They said they'd ring up at the pay phone down the street in," Rick checked his gold wristwatch, "twenty minutes, so we better go."

Coffee in hand, Miller circled the table until he stood at the windows overlooking the rear patio and carefully manicured garden. No alley beyond that he could see, just the windowless flank of the neighboring building, but the high wall bordering the garden had a small gate notched into its east side. The gate had to lead somewhere.

A chair creaked. Rick whispered something to Lady Hardy before padding into the hallway, followed by Scott. Miller was alone with the ancient woman.

"Nice place," he told her, turning around. "If you're in trouble, just blink. It's okay, you can let me know. I'm one of the nice ones."

No reply from the lady.

"Thanks for the coffee," he said, setting down the cup, and left the room.

Out in the foyer, Scott and Rick had slipped on their shoes. Miller stepped past them and opened the front door, planning on exiting the building first. He had never worked as a bodyguard before, but how hard could it be? Just hurt anyone who looked at your client funny.

The kid with the red cap stood on the sidewalk, only instead of a ball, he held a silver pistol that seemed almost as large as he was. Miller grinned, ready to say something witty—*Heck of a toy, kid*—except the pistol didn't look like a toy at all, it looked heavy and metallic and real as the kid leveled it at Miller's head, and Miller dodged to the left, but instead of swinging the barrel to follow him, the kid kept it pointed at the door as his finger squeezed the trigger.

And then everything went to hell.

CHAPTER 7

THE KID'S PISTOL SPAT FLAME, THE ROUND SNAPPING PAST MILLER'S head. Miller had his left hand in his jacket pocket, finger tightening on the trigger of the .38. It was a cliché to say that time stretched out during combat, that your speeding brain had what felt like eons to consider all the angles and possibilities, but there was some meat in the truism. The kid seemed to take forever to swivel on his heel, the pistol sweeping toward Miller at such a glacial pace that he could debate his next move. Could he shoot a child?

No. He had rules against putting a round in an ankle-biter's skull. The knee, though…

Miller squeezed the trigger and his jacket pocket burst, scattering bits of charred fabric. The kid screamed and clutched his leg, dropping the pistol.

Miller felt quite pleased with himself. Neutralize the target without killing. He just needed to wrestle the little bastard to the sidewalk and figure out why he was trying to turn this quiet stretch of Irving Place into a shooting gallery—

The kid stumbled backward into the street. A metallic flash in the corner of Miller's eye, a rising roar as a truck barreled through, smashing into the kid and sending him flying into the air like a football. The truck's brakes screeched.

There was nobody on the sidewalk. The shooting,

followed by the kid's subsequent pancaking, had taken place in those rare moments when a New York City street was absent of foot traffic. What luck. Miller sprinted up the townhouse steps, intent on disappearing inside before the truck driver saw him, only to stop in the open doorway.

Rick was dead.

The kid's bullet had smashed him in the chest. He lay in the foyer, his blank eyes fixed on the ceiling. Scott knelt beside him, weeping into his hands.

A crying lawyer, Miller thought. That's a first.

"I don't understand," Scott murmured between sobs. "I don't understand…"

"Rick piss off any kids lately?" Miller asked, slamming the door behind him.

"What?"

"Kid with a gun outside. Red hat. Rick take his lunch money or something?" Miller stripped off the jacket with its shredded pocket and dropped it on the floor, setting the warm .38 atop it. The .25 was a small gun and he slipped it into the left pocket of his jeans, pulling out his shirt so the hem covered part of the bulge.

"What?"

Miller grabbed Scott's collar. "Did you see the kid? His pistol was bigger than he was."

"Why would a kid shoot Rick?"

"Excellent question." With his free hand, Miller checked his watch, surprised at how little time had passed since he stepped outside. "There's another fifteen minutes until Rick's contact rings that phone booth. I figure we better be there to answer."

"But…"

"No 'but.' How much money is the deal worth?"

"A hundred thousand."

"What the hell was Rick up to?"

"I don't know. He wouldn't tell me anything except it was big." Scott began to babble. "But if he's dead then what do we do, we can't do anything if he's dead, they won't meet with us if he's dead…"

"Shut up."

Scott's mouth snapped closed.

Miller crunched numbers. He would take almost all of the money, of course. Scott could have a small finder's fee, maybe twenty grand. "These people, you never dealt with them yourself?"

"No."

That was a problem, but not an impossible one. "Fine. Which phone booth? The one on the Square, on 15th?"

"Yes." Scott stared into Rick's dead face as if it held all the answers.

"I'll be back." Retrieving his ruined jacket and the .38, Miller walked through the house, past the silent Lady Hardy, and out the doors off the dining room onto the back patio. He tossed the jacket and the pistol behind a thick tangle of brush before jogging to the garden gate, which was locked. Slotting his feet into its cast-iron curves, he vaulted over, finding himself in an alley so narrow its walls scraped his shoulders as he made his way toward the street. The alley's opening ended in another gate, taller but unlocked when he tried the knob.

The alley was a little south of the house, which placed him further away from the scene brewing around the truck down the street. A cop cruiser had arrived. Looky-loos congregated around the kid's body. What kind of child could commit murder? There'd been little time for a good look at the kid's face, but Miller remembered how the eyes had the professional coldness of a lifelong hitman.

Miller walked to Union Square, pausing on the corner of 15th and Union Square East to survey the scene. It was still too early for much street life but a busker with a battered banjo leaned against the stone wall surrounding the central park, a stained hat with a few quarters between his feet. A few hustlers snoozed against the fence surrounding the George Washington statue at the square's southern end, which Miller took as a sign that no cops lurked nearby.

Satisfied with the setup, Miller crossed the street. A thickly bearded man in a stained sport jacket paced in front of the phone booth he needed, muttering rhythmically under his breath.

"Excuse me," Miller said, pointing at the booth.

"We're the lost tribes of the crazed scribblers," the poet informed him. "We're sprawled on the Hudson's rocky edge, pissing our precious words into the abyss."

"A masterpiece," Miller said. "But I have a call to make."

"And as we piss, we dance, and as we dance, we tell the people all the most valuable things, which are nothing, and that is zero is hip." The poet flashed yellow teeth. "Absolute zero is as hip as it'll ever get."

Miller debated slamming the poet's head into the side of the booth. A tempting prospect, but it would bring too much attention. He still felt shaky from the shooting. A few inches to the left or right, and the kid might have blown his head off.

Miller placed a gentle hand on the poet's shoulder. "Go sprawl somewhere else," he said.

"Destroyed," the poet said, warming to his theme. "Destroyed on your mother's floor, destroyed on the fiery streets where the souls burn up, destroyed in the forest." But he moved away, drifting up the stone steps to Union Square's grassy heart.

Tucked into the booth, Miller stacked dimes atop the phone and placed the receiver to his ear, miming a call. In his free hand, he held his handkerchief.

At twenty seconds to the appointed minute he hung up the receiver and waited. The phone rang right on time. A good sign. Pressing the handkerchief over the mouthpiece, he grunted, "Yes?"

"Rick?" A man's voice, deep, with a slight accent, definitely European, maybe German. Despite his adventures overseas, Miller had no ear for accents.

"Yes, this is he." It was hard to imitate Rick's high notes, but Miller grimaced and did his best.

A pause, so long Miller feared the man would hang up.

"Riis Park boardwalk," the man finally said. "Wise and Son Clock. They also call it the Wise Clock. Wednesday. Midnight. Come alone with the item, Rick, you understand, yes?"

"Yes."

The click of disconnection.

Miller hung up the phone and stared through the booth's windows at the passing cars. This time yesterday, he had been sitting in his apartment, luxuriating in the release of tension that always came after the completion of a job. His only plans had involved a few beers at McSorley's. Yesterday seemed like a million years ago.

The poet drifted into view again, shouting now, his words distorted by the booth's scarred glass: "Who jumped off the skyscrapers, who jumped onto their knives, who jumped when they fired the gun, who walked through fire, and who finally realized the worth of zero, which is everything…"

Miller shuddered. He knew too many people who died from knives and guns and jumping off tall buildings.

When he finally shuffled off this mortal coil, who would remember him?

Before walking back to Rick's mansion, he gave the poet the rest of his phone dimes. "Don't wake at the police," the poet told him.

"I'll keep it in mind," Miller said.

The truck and cop cruiser still sat at the end of Rick's street, surrounded by a shrinking crowd. He ducked through the gate, climbed into the backyard, and spent a minute digging a shallow hole beneath a rose bush. He retrieved the .38 from its hiding place and dropped it into the hole and shoved dirt over it. What a pity to bury the weapon after spending so much on it, but he could always dig it up once the cops lost interest in the kid's death.

With the ruined jacket folded over his arm, he re-entered the house through the dining room. Lady Hardy might have shifted an inch or two since he left, but it was hard to tell. In the foyer, he found Scott hunched over Rick's body, his fingers trembling as he adjusted the collar of Rick's blood-spattered shirt over and over again.

"They called," Miller said.

Scott wiped his nose with the back of his hand. "And?"

"Meeting is at Riis Beach. Wednesday. They wanted Rick to come alone."

"Well." Scott laughed without a trace of humor. "How are we going to pull that off?"

"That's our first worry. The caller also said something about an item. You have any idea about that?"

"No. Can we…" A loud sniff. "Please, he's dead. I can't…"

"Don't worry, we'll figure it out," Miller said, peeking through the curtained front windows. Two bored officers leaned against the police cruiser. From this angle, he could see the ambulance parked in front of the truck, and the kid covered in a white sheet. "We have to deal with Rick's body. I assume a big house like this has a big refrigerator or freezer. Take me to it."

CHAPTER 8

AFTER THEY LOADED RICK'S BODY INTO THE WALK-IN REFRIGERATOR IN the basement, they retreated to the enormous kitchen so Miller could make himself a fresh cup of coffee. He still felt shaky, his muscles weak. Coffee was a poor substitute for the pills he sometimes took on overnight jobs, but it would power him through the next few hours.

As Scott washed his face in one of the kitchen sinks, Miller said, "I'll be back Wednesday afternoon."

Scott spat water. "What am I supposed to do until then?"

The time for coddling was over. "Search Rick's things. Search the house. Whatever this 'item' is, we need to find it."

"What could it be?"

"No idea. Documents, or photographs, or anything worth an insane amount of money."

"Aren't you sad Rick's dead? He was your friend."

"Sure, I'm sad he's dead. But you know what will make me sadder?"

"Not getting Rick's money from the deal?"

"Exactly."

"You're a harsh bastard."

"It's a harsh world. The other night, I asked Rick how he ended up in this house, and he said something about 'dashing good looks.' What did he mean by that?"

Scott buried his face in a towel, his voice muffled. "Rick met Lady Hardy at a society event about a year ago. At that time, we needed a place to live, so he, ah, persuaded her to let us stay here." A deep breath through damp cloth. "And he was very persuasive, believe me."

"Lady Hardy speaks?"

"Yes, of course. And at night she roars, if you catch my drift." Scott dropped the towel in the sink, his face twisted in misery.

"If Rick's dead, will she let you stay here?"

"I could tell her Rick's on a trip for a few days, sure, but at some point, her hunger would grow too great." Scott sighed. "Then I'll need a new place to live."

"If we do this deal, maybe you'll be able to buy a house of your own."

"They're expecting to deal with Rick."

"We'll figure it out," Rick said, and slugged down the boiling coffee in one gulp. "Wednesday afternoon." Setting the cup on the counter, he left Scott to his grief.

Down the street, the police cruiser and the ambulance had left. *You need to figure out about that kid*, Miller told himself as he headed south, his jacket draped over his arm. *The kid was aiming at Rick. I bet the murder had to do with the deal. But where do I start?*

Only one destination would do.

There was another bar he frequented off Union Square, a dark-walled dive named Kraven's, where he knew the bartender would let him use the phone so long as he kept buying beers and food. He arrived as it was opening and ordered a beer. The bartender set the phone beside Miller's glass without him needing to ask.

He dialed a number. Three rings and a woman answered: "Hello?"

"It's me."

A sharp intake of breath. "Are you in jail?"

"No, thanks for asking." He unfolded the jacket and

poked a finger through the hole left by the .38. "I do need your help, though."

Her voice dropped. There must have been people in the office with her. "What?"

"I need to get into the morgue."

A sigh. "Really? You don't talk to me for a month, then you ring up, all casual, and say you need… that? Why?"

"There's a body in there I need to see."

"Why?"

"That part's not important to you. Can you do it?"

"I don't even know where to start with you."

"Start by saying 'yes.' I'll take you to dinner afterward."

"You're such a caveman."

"I take that as a complement."

Another sigh, louder. "Okay, fine. When are you coming down?"

"Right now."

"Great. Thanks for giving me some warning."

"See you in thirty." He hung up. She had agreed to dinner, at least. Who had picked up the phone when he called her apartment earlier? Did it matter? She deserved better than someone who disappeared every few months, who earned his money through criminal means. But he knew that part of him excited her, too.

CHAPTER 9

JILL RILEY STOOD ON THE SIDEWALK IN FRONT OF THE OFFICE OF THE Medical Examiner, a half-smoked cigarette between her lips. She wore a dark red dress and high heels. Her red hair was done up in a tight bun. When she saw Miller walking up the street, she waggled her fingers at him, her face grim.

"It's good to see you," he said, and meant it. Before meeting her, he had returned to his apartment to drop off his ruined jacket and change into a nice brown suit with a white shirt and dark tie. With his trim moustache and blonde hair chopped tight against his skull, he could have been a salesman who boxed on the weekends. It was good camouflage, the pants draping neatly over his ankle holster with the .25.

She dropped the cigarette and ground it beneath her heel. "Someplace fancy," she said.

"What?"

"For dinner tonight. Someplace fancy. With actual tablecloths and candles. I mean it."

"I can do that."

"Good, and I'll hold you to that. We're going through a side entrance. Before we do that, what exactly are we looking for?"

"A child was brought in, hit by a truck. About two hours ago, maybe."

She shuddered. "Christ, that's awful."

"I'd be inclined to agree with you, except the kid fired a gun in my direction."

"Part of me wants to ask, and part of me doesn't."

"Better that you don't. Can we go inside?"

She led him through an entrance that opened onto a long hallway, white and bright and pungent with disinfectant. They took a left into a storeroom, where she fished a white lab jacket from a bin. "Everyone knows everyone here," she said. "If someone questions you, you're a visiting doctor. Try to act like one."

He slipped on the lab jacket. It was a tight fit over his clothes. He placed a hand on her hip. "Thank you," he said.

She stepped back, letting his hand fall away. "Don't thank me yet. This might get me in a lot of trouble."

"That's why I thanked you."

"And you haven't called in so long. You just disappear, then you come back and you need something."

"When haven't I made it up to you?"

"At some point, that won't work anymore. Let's get this done." Exiting the storeroom, she led him down the hallway and through more doors, until they stood inside a cold chamber lined with metal tables. Each table had a sheet-wrapped body on it, the bloodless feet poking out.

"Make it quick," she said. "People are in and out of here all the time."

It was easy to spot the right body, which only took up half of its assigned table. The tag attached to one of the tiny toes read: "Unknown." He paused to examine the feet. The bottoms were rough and cracked, the skin budding with callouses. Not like young feet at all.

He whipped the sheet back. The kid's face, hidden by his red cap during the encounter in the street, was fully revealed in the milky light from overhead. He had bony cheeks and tanned, lined skin, along with hair too thin and dry for anyone under the age of forty.

"Wow, that kid lived hard," Jill said.

"He was a pretty good shot, too." Miller peeled back the boy's upper lip, revealing teeth stained brown from either coffee or tobacco. The truck's impact had cracked the jaw, but otherwise the head seemed untouched. The chest was bruised, the ribs caved in.

"There," Miller said, touching a discoloration above the left nipple, on the edge of the bruising. It was a tattoo, a curling snake with batwings poking from its back. Maybe it was a dragon. In any case, the ink was old, blurring into the skin.

"You got what you need?" Jill gave the door a significant look.

"Almost done." Miller found where the bullet from his .38 had creased the kid's knee without lodging in the flesh. Good. With any luck, the spent round was lost forever in the gutter. He could dig up the .38 without worrying about the cops tying it to the shooting.

Dragging the sheet over the strange face, he said, "Is there a box or something with his clothes?"

"Yes, but not here." She pulled him into the hallway. "And it's too risky for you to go into that area, so just leave me to it and I'll see what I can find…"

A man in a white lab jacket approached them at high speed, a clipboard clutched in his hand. With his chin tilted at an imperial angle, and his eyes squinting down his nose, he reminded Miller of every bureaucrat and limp-dick lieutenant he ever had the misfortune of encountering. "Jill," the man said, his tone conveying threat. "Jill, how many times did I ask you…"

"They're filed," Jill snapped. "We're following the new filing system."

The man's lips writhed in barely contained rage, spittle flying as he snarled, "I didn't ask you about the new filing system. I couldn't care about the filing system. When I say I want a file, I want a file on my desk right now, do you understand…"

"Yes." Jill's eyes flicked to the floor.

"Good. Who is this?"

"Doctor Johnson." Miller could lie as smoothly as butter sliding down a hot pan.

"I'm Doctor Richards, medical examiner. Doctor Johnson from where? I don't know you."

"Jersey City Hospital." Miller smiled at Jill. "Just here to visit my friend."

"You shouldn't be visiting her down here. This is off-limits to everyone but staff. You'd expect Jill here to know that, since she's a secretary." Richards pumped all the venom he could into the last word.

"We'll be on our way, then." Miller stuck out his hand to shake, and Richards instinctively reached out to take it. The doctor's hand was soft. Miller squeezed as hard as he could. Richards looked surprised, then pained, as he tried to pull his hand back.

Miller gripped harder. "Nothing about your degree gives you the right to treat Jill here with anything less than respect. Do you understand?"

Richards whined: "You can't…"

"I certainly can." Miller twisted the hand so hard the wrist threatened to break, forcing Richards to one knee. "Do you understand?"

"Yes!"

Miller kept the pressure on. "One other thing. As I recall,

Jill isn't a secretary, she's a medical examiner assistant. You'll address her as such. Is that clear?"

"Yes!"

"Good." Miller released the hand, and Richards sank back on his haunches. "I don't need to tell you what might happen if you try to report this."

Without waiting for a reply, Miller placed a hand on Jill's back, escorting her around the whining doctor. As they passed the storeroom, he shrugged off the lab jacket and placed it on the doorknob. Outside again, they paused on the sidewalk so Jill could light a fresh cigarette.

"Thank you," she said, her face reddening. "What you did to him was really quite something."

"You're welcome. Let me know if he tries anything again."

"Yes, yes, of course." She squeezed his forearm. "Dinner, and we'll put all this behind us."

CHAPTER 10

THE STRAND BOOKSTORE HAD SAT ON THE CORNER OF EAST 12TH AND Broadway for three years, since moving from its old location on Fourth Avenue. Occupying the building's wide first floor, it was one of the few survivors of what had once been Book Row, a glorious stretch of bookstores strangled by the Great Depression. Miller drifted in, perusing the front shelves until he caught the eye of the fellow working the register, who nodded and pointed at the front door.

Outside again, Miller waited beneath the Strand's red awning. He thought about Jill and how badly she wanted to become a medical examiner. She had even tracked down Frances Glessner Lee, the mother of forensic science, for lessons in how to best observe a corpse's details. Jill liked to talk about Lee's dollhouses, the Nutshell Studies of Unexplained Death, each portraying a murder scene in miniature. You could learn a lot about death by studying the tiny corpses in their chaotic rooms.

Despite her efforts, the usual forces had killed Jill's dreams. Lack of money. Lack of time. Too many pricks like Richards who couldn't see women for their brains. Thinking about it made Miller wish he'd broken Richards in half.

The fellow from the register stepped outside and lit a cigarette. He was all gray hair and bony angles, his lips bent in a wry smirk. He wore a black shirt and a pair of jeans splattered with red, white, and black paint. The nametag on his chest said: "Bob."

"Sergeant," Bob said.

"Corporal," Miller returned.

"Been a long time."

"That hair isn't regulation." Miller grinned. "The pants, either."

"I'm trying to become a painter. Little bit of abstraction, like Jackson Pollock." Bob cocked an eyebrow. "What do you think of that?"

"You're not doing tattoos anymore?"

"No, I gave that up. Besides, that shop where I was working out of, down on West 4th? Those fellows were getting a little odd. Why do you ask? You finally in the mood for some ink?"

"Not me, no." No tattoos made it harder to identify you. "But I have a question about one I saw."

"Yeah?"

Miller drew a scrap of paper from his pocket. After leaving the morgue, he had done his best to sketch the winged snake on the kid's body. He handed it to Bob, who held it at arm's length as he squinted through his smoke.

"Sure, I've seen that before." Bob handed it back. "You have, too, I think. In France, right after we reached Paris, in that café?"

"I don't remember."

"Actually, maybe you weren't there. There was a weird man there, like a midget. I forget his name. He said he had some condition, I think it was called hypo… hypo… hypo-something. Made him look like a kid even though he was a fully grown adult. Yeah, you weren't there, because you would've remembered how he got up on the bar and slugged down a whole bottle of whiskey that was big as he was."

"Was the midget French?"

"No, American. We used him for all types of spy and sabotage work, they told me. It's easy to sneak into places when you look like a child. I heard they sent him to burn down this whorehouse in Paris with a bunch of Nazi commanders inside. Anyway, he had that tattoo on his chest. It was brand new, so he was showing it off to everyone."

"You know what happened to him?"

A tapping on the storefront window behind them. Bob turned and made a just-one-minute signal to whoever waited on the other side. "Why you so interested?" he asked.

"He took a shot at me. Then got hit by a car. He's dead."

Bob dropped his cigarette and crushed it under his heel. "Life's a very odd thing. You know why he wanted you dead?"

"No. I had no idea who he was. But I saw that tattoo. I figured I'd ask a tattoo artist."

"Listen, let me ask around a bit. I still have connections with the spooks from back in the day. They might know something that could help out."

"That would be ideal." Miller drew his roll of bills from his pocket and peeled off a twenty. "For art supplies."

"Much appreciated. You got a number I can call?"

Miller gave him the number at Kraven's. "Leave a message there."

"Will do." Bob, opening the bookstore's door, paused to look in the direction of Union Square. Miller followed Bob's gaze. On the corner, the grimy poet who accosted Miller at the phone booth was holding court with the pigeons, waving his arms as he screamed:

"Who were wrecked in your father's attic, and wrecked in the Pentagon, and wrecked in the socialist jungles…"

Miller shook his head. "Saw him before. Crazy."

"Well," Bob said, "I guess we're all one bad week away from that. Word to the wise, that midget was probably involved in big trouble. You watch yourself."

During the war, Bob had killed like an unstoppable machine. Miller once watched as Bob climbed aboard a burning M10 tank destroyer and used its abandoned .50 caliber to massacre a squad of German soldiers crawling toward him through the forest. Books and movies always suggested violence hardened you up, made you a more effective killer, and yet Miller had seen nothing in real life to prove that idea. Having ripped his way across Europe, Bob wanted to hide from his demons in a forest of books and art. Miller understood.

CHAPTER 11

BEFORE MILLER WENT TO DINNER WITH JILL, HE SWUNG BY RICK'S MAN- sion and found Scott in front of the fireplace, polishing off a bottle of gin without a glass, Colonel Longshanks crumpled at his feet.

"I say, sir, we didn't expect you until the day after tomorrow," Scott said in Colonel Longshank's voice. The alcohol made the accent sloppy.

"You got to have your hand up the puppet's ass for it to be convincing," Miller said. "Rick was stateside during the war, right?"

"Yeah, he was 4F. God knows how he managed that. Say whatever you will about him, he was good at putting one over on people."

"He was at that. Was he ever in France or Germany, after the war?"

"You were his friend, so your guess is as good as mine. I don't think he really had any urge to leave the country. Why do you ask?"

I suppose I didn't really know Rick at all, Miller thought. A few weeks in New Orleans, a few days in San Francisco—it's amazing how little time it takes to think you have someone's whole story. "Tell you later, maybe," he said. "You go through Rick's things?"

Scott nodded, and his voice caught. "It was… hard."

"You find anything that could be our item?"

"No. Rick didn't have much stuff. His suits, his toiletries, some books and tools. There was nothing he hadn't had with him for a long time."

"Okay." Miller made a note to search through Rick's things later, on his own. Maybe it would take an outsider's eyes to see what Scott, in his grief, had missed. Turning to leave, he spun again. "Question," he said.

"What? You want to know Rick's shoe size?"

"No. A good restaurant around here. Fancy. Where would you go?"

"Fancy? Around Union Square? That's quite a heavy lift." Scott sucked air through his teeth. "There's a decent steakhouse over on University and 12th if you're looking for meat. It's called 'The Golden Bull.' The décor is traditional, a little boring, but you strike me as someone who isn't into *nouveau*."

Miller had never heard of the place. "That will work."

The Golden Bull was exactly as Scott described. The dim lighting gave it a cavernous feel, and nobody had bothered to update the furniture since Teddy Roosevelt's administration. The waiters treated Jill like a queen after seating them in a rear booth. Jill ordered a martini while Miller opted for a beer.

"You realize I'm a vegetarian, right?" Jill frowned at the next table, where a trio of businessmen tore into hunks of bloody meat.

"What's a vegetarian?"

Her frown transformed into a smirk. "You're kidding."

"So are you."

"Damnit."

"What?"

"I can never get one over on you."

"I wouldn't let it keep you up at night."

"Did you get what you needed today?"

"I did, thank you."

"But you won't tell me what you were looking for. Why you had me sneak you into the morgue to look at a kid with a weird face."

"A midget."

"What?"

"It's better if you don't know."

"Why?"

"Less danger."

Their drinks arrived, and they both ordered steaks with mashed potatoes. Jill had an enormous appetite for everything: food, cigarettes, conversation, sex. It was one of the many things Miller liked about her.

Jill ran her finger around the lip of her glass. "At what point do you tell me?"

"About what I do?"

"Yes. Don't get me wrong, I love this thing we have, but it's not sustainable. It goes on longer, and we're partners. I'm not talking marriage or anything like that. But there needs to be more…"

"What?"

"I'm trying to think of the word. Openness, I guess. Trust. I'm a big girl. I can take the danger."

"Can you?"

"Let me tell you a story. When I was a little girl, my father owned a slaughterhouse. Did I ever tell you about that? No, I don't think I did. It's not exactly the sort of tale you share with a man on your first few dates. I was always so curious about what exactly my father did for a living, how," she tipped her glass at the neighboring table and its grilled meats, "all that beautiful steak ended up on our dinner table at night."

"Did he take you?"

"No, not at first. He thought it'd be too bloody for me. 'It's not for a little missus like you,' he'd say, and waggle his finger at me. Then I got into a fight with my brother Drew. A bad one, right in our driveway. I had the aggression, but Drew had the size, and he threw me to the ground. I was on my back, trying to kick him, when my father drove up in his big Buick.

"I thought he'd punish Drew, but that wasn't the case at all, oh no. My father grabbed me by my shoulders and hauled me upright, and—I'll never forget this—he got down until we were eye-to-eye and yelled: 'Don't you ever fight like that. Only an animal fights on its back.' I'd never seen him so mad. Seeing me like that must have sparked some memory, is all I can figure.

"Then he bundled me into the car. I didn't know where we were going. When we got to the slaughterhouse, I was scared, but I was also excited, because I'd wanted to go there for so long. I was a very strange little girl in a lot of ways. He dragged me out and took me right to the killing floor. The smell was intense. These men stood on the line with sledgehammers, and every time a cow came down, they would take a swing, whack, and smash its brains in."

"Your father sounds like quite the charmer."

"He was raised rough. I don't blame him. He walked the line with me, showing how they stripped all that cattle into beef. And at the end of it, once we were back in the car, he said: 'Little scrub, you have two choices in life. You can either be the cow, or the man with the sledgehammer.' We drove back to the house, and Drew was standing there in the driveway, just where we left him. My father said, 'I want you to go out there and punch your brother in the face.'"

Miller chuckled. "What'd you do?"

"What do you think? I got out of the car and socked Drew in the nose. And Drew never tried to hit me again. You know why I'm telling you this story?"

Miller shrugged.

"Because I decided that I was going to be the person with the sledgehammer. And you, you're a sledgehammer man. That's why we get along." She reached across the table and took his hand. "That's why I can take it. Whenever you're ready."

"The midget," he said.

"Yes. The midget. Tell me of the midget's ways, O Great One."

"He took a shot at me this morning, when I was standing outside a friend's house. I don't know why. I figured I could learn something in the morgue." He sipped his beer. "Turns out, that tattoo on his chest was from the war. But that's all I have."

"I take it midgets shooting at you isn't a normal thing?"

"It was my first time. With midgets, at least."

"It didn't have anything to do with your regular job."

"No."

"The job you won't tell me about."

"The job, it pays well, when it pays. I'm an entrepreneur, let's say, and leave it at that."

"Ooh, 'entrepreneur,' fancy term."

"It's close enough." He paused, thinking about last night in McSorley's, alone with his beer. He was happy with his life, wasn't he? What would his life look like with a full-time woman in it?

"So can we?" Her face soft in the dimness.

"Can we what?"

"Get a little more serious."

She couldn't betray what she knew nothing about. He would need to establish firm lines. "We can."

"Good. So are you an 'entrepreneur' like Al Capone, or an 'entrepreneur' like John Dillinger?" She smiled.

"Capone or Dillinger?" He smiled back, despite his stomach feeling like an elevator with the cables cut. "Neither. Both of them way too theatrical. If you want to survive in a business like mine, you need to be cool, professional."

"Man of few words."

"Exactly."

"I think you've said more words to me in the past ten minutes than you did during our first two dates. What other surprises do you have in store?"

Their steaks arrived, sizzling and smoking. Jill made a show of hefting the blade, playing with its weight, before she began to slice flesh. Miller started with his potatoes, trying to feel at ease. When they finished dinner, and Jill disappeared into the bathroom for a few minutes, he used his napkin to wipe the fingerprints off his silverware. Old habit.

CHAPTER **12**

FULL OF MEAT AND ALCOHOL, THEY STUMBLED TO HIS PLACE. NO SOONER had he flicked on the light and shut the door when the old man upstairs commenced his furious rocking.

Creak-creak-creak-creak.

Jill, shedding her jacket, looked at the ceiling and said, "What the hell is that?"

"Old man up there," Miller said, opening his cabinets. He had a bottle of good whiskey around here, didn't he? It was Jill's first time in the apartment, and he felt a twinge of embarrassment at his almost-empty cabinets, the rooms lacking furniture or art on the walls. He had always taken pride in his lack of attachments and possessions. Would a woman look at it the same way?

"What's his problem?" Hopping from one foot to the other, Jill kicked her shoes into the corner.

"I don't know. Never met him. Never spoken to him. I just know he's old because that's what the landlady said. But he sure loves annoying me with that rocking chair."

"Maybe he's trying to send you a signal. Like in code." Tilting her head to the ceiling, she shouted, "Two creaks for 'yes,' one creak for 'no,' please."

The rocking stopped.

"That ought to do it, hopefully. Thank you for finally

inviting me over." She spun on her heel. "It is very… monastic."

In the cabinet over the sink, Miller found a dusty bottle of very fine single malt, his loot from a bad night in Chinatown a year before. It had a bit of dried blood crusted on the neck, which he wiped off before setting it on the counter. As he fetched two glasses, he said, "I'm not home often."

"No, it's fine. I could do with less stuff, myself."

Creak-creak-creak-creak.

Miller pictured a lightning bolt shooting from the top of his head, through the ceiling, and incinerating the old man in his irritating chair. Like something a Greek God would do to a peasant who was preventing him from mating with a beautiful swan. Wasn't that how the legend went? He was a little drunk.

Jill laughed. "You have to admit, it's sort of funny."

"Sure, unless I'm trying to sleep." Miller returned to the bedroom with the bottle and glasses.

Jill sat on the edge of the bed. "I don't think we'll get a lot of sleep tonight."

She was right. And for the rest of the night, Miller gave himself permission to forget about everything: the dead midget, his former partners coming to kill him, and especially the old man creaking away the time above their heads.

CHAPTER 13

BERNARD AND TRENT PUMPED THE CLOWN FULL OF LEAD, BUT THE CLOWN never relaxed. Arms spread, the clown floated above the fair, his shadow drifting over the crowd's upturned faces.

Trent whooped as he fired into Miller's empty hand, a wave of pain dampening Miller's cry. Something big and black and shaking slammed into Miller, jerking him backward. He stood beside a brick wall with a ladder bolted to it, which he climbed as fast as he could. He made it to the roof before he collapsed, choking on his own blood.

"It's okay," the clown said, floating high above. "It's just an error. Error overflow. Error."

Miller clenched his jaw and tried to rise again.

"Error," the clown said through bloody teeth. "Memory error."

The roof was a parking lot, with a few red-and-blue lights twinkling in the distance. In the middle of the space stood a burned-out trash can. Miller walked over to it, knowing that blackened cylinder held his pistol, hat, ammunition, and two duffel bags.

Bernard and Trent hadn't reached the roof yet, and the clown was still yelling about errors. Miller had one thing on his mind: escape. The trash can bloomed flame. Miller's veins screamed for him to do something, anything. He was too late. Too much heat. Smell the burning.

Miller climbed into the trash can and sat in the flames, chin on chest, trying to think of something else to do. In the middle of the parking lot stood Bob, shaking like a leaf. Miller made a deep, sad sound. Bob stared at him, saying nothing.

Maybe this didn't go as planned, Miller thought. Maybe I ruined it all—

CHAPTER **14**

IN THE MORNING, MILLER'S HEAD THROBBED LIKE A CRACKED TOOTH. HE took Jill to the nearest café for coffee. It was a place he visited often. He was more aware than usual of the passerby marching past the plate-glass windows, the tinkling of the bell every time the door opened. There was simply no way Bernard and Trent could have reached New York by this point, right?

A hell of a dream last night. Miller had snapped awake with tears rolling down his cheeks. He felt like his instincts were off, that his ability to calculate danger had frayed at the edges. Sitting with his back to the café's rear wall, angled slightly so he could see past Jill to the front door and the street beyond, he kept his left hand on his thigh, close to the pocket where he kept the .25.

Once their coffees arrived, he told her, "Let me know if that doctor gives you grief today."

She shook her head. "No, he's a coward. I wouldn't worry about it."

"Do you like working there?"

"Do I like the medical examiner's office? Yes. Do I like my job? No. In another life, I would have gone to school to become a medical examiner." She shrugged.

"I bet you could do a hell of an autopsy."

"I could have cause of death pinned down in no time at all."

"What's stopping you?"

"From doing an autopsy? They don't appreciate it when a clerk grabs a knife and starts dicing up the stiffs."

"I meant from becoming a medical examiner."

"You know."

"I want you to say it."

"Why?"

"Trust me."

"Because it's a man's institution. You should hear how they talk to me."

"I got a taste of it with that fellow whose hand I almost broke. If you had the right degrees, would that change?"

"Maybe. It'd be a rough journey, and I'd take a lot of grief, but maybe you could help me. Stand by my shoulder, crack a skull every time someone says something sore."

"I'd be happy to."

"But degrees cost money."

"They do at that." He poured more sugar into his cup. "They do at that."

He dropped her off at the subway before walking to Kraven's, where he banged on the door until the bartender, who slept on a mattress in the back, opened it an inch.

"You have a message for me?" Miller said. "From Bob?"

The bartender, nonplussed, passed a torn scrap of paper through the gap before locking the door again.

Miller unfolded the message. 'Midget Location,' it read, below an address off 2nd and 10th. Walking there, Miller discovered it was a four-story apartment building a few decades past its best days: cracked brick, dust-smeared windows, a front door with a broken lock. He pushed the door open and entered a dirty hallway strewn with cigarette butts and yellowing fliers. A narrow staircase led to the fourth floor.

If the address was correct, the midget lived in 4F. Miller found the door and twisted the knob. Locked. The door itself was cheap wood, poorly painted and scratched. It was also loose in its frame. Taking a step back, Miller drove his foot into the lock an inch below the knob. The door cracked and shuddered open.

The apartment was minimalist, reminding Miller in some ways of his own. The kitchen was bare, the small counters covered with a thin layer of dust. The bedroom was likewise empty except for a small wooden desk and a child's cot pushed into one corner, below a small, framed photograph of the Eiffel Tower.

He opened the desk's single drawer, revealing a half-empty pack of gum, a blank pad of paper, some paperclips, and a collection of stubby pencils. On a hunch, he placed the pad on the desk and lightly rubbed the tip of the pencil over the top sheet, revealing a series of pale lines against the spreading gray. He knew from reading pulp magazines that writing on a pad with a pen or pencil sometimes left indentations two or three sheets deep, depending on how hard you pressed, and you could summon those words with some lightly applied graphite.

Letters swam from the gray, in two rows:

SVRNC5
SEOIA7

A code of some sort. He tore away the pad's top four sheets and pocketed them before resuming his search. The wall opposite the cot was light green with a darker patch in the middle of it, a square measuring an arm's length by an arm's length. He waved his hand over the square, thinking it was maybe a trick of the light filtering through the dusty window. His passing shadow failed to obliterate it. A painting or photograph had hung there once, preventing the sun from bleaching the paint beneath.

Miller moved on. The bathroom had been converted to a darkroom, with a red bulb screwed into the fixture. Sheets covered the small window above the tub. Photographs hung on a clothesline strung between the showerhead and the cabinet. He squinted at them in the bloody light. Each image framed a different section of beach: a sandy road cutting through small trees, a lighthouse, a black mass that could have been a rock, bear, or a mistake in the film development.

He plucked the photographs from the line and slipped them into his jacket pocket. Maybe they would mean something to Bob or Scott.

From far below, a door slammed. Heavy footsteps echoed in the stairwell. He sensed trouble. Time to leave. He walked to the bedroom. A security gate blocked the window. He flipped open the cover over the gate's latch. Secured with a padlock. The apartment's front door was his only route out.

In the hallway, he peeked down the stairwell. A shadow drifted across the walls as whoever was down there made their way up. If it was more than one person, he needed to meet them in the stairwell, box them in.

He wrapped his hand around the .25 in his pocket as he started down the stairs. On the third-floor landing stood a blonde man, big and square, dressed in a brown leather jacket and loose jeans. The man's blue eyes locked on Miller. The man's hand drifted into his jacket pocket.

CHAPTER 15

THE MAN ASKED, "ARE YOU POLICE?" HIS VOICE WAS LIGHTLY ACCENTED, familiar somehow.

Miller shook his head. His finger rested on the trigger of the .25.

"That is good." The man offered a little smile.

Miller waited another quarter-second, until man's hand began to re-emerge from his pocket. A flash of steel. Handle, cylinder, hammer. Gun.

Miller pulled the trigger.

The .25 clicked.

Misfire. First damn time with this gun.

He would have died in the next moment except the man at the bottom of the stairs cared about his beautiful leather jacket, spent too long drawing the pistol instead of firing through the pocket. The hammer snagged on the lining and the man yanked at it, his face twisting in irritation.

Miller leapt.

It was maybe fifteen feet vertical, ten feet horizontal from the fourth-floor landing to the third. More than enough distance to break a leg if you landed wrong. Miller's knee rammed into the man's sternum hard enough to crack bone. The man crashed backward into the wall.

Miller tumbled away, his tailbone colliding with a step,

his spine sparkling with pain. The man bounced off the wall and stumbled forward, his chin spotted with blood, his hand clutching an FN Model 1922 semi-automatic pistol.

Miller lashed out with his right foot, striking the man's knee. With a gurgle, the man dropped the pistol and fell sideways, somersaulting down the stairs to the second floor. More bones cracked. Miller crawled to the edge of the landing in time to see the man smack into the wall on the second-floor landing, bounce, and roll down the stairs to the first.

Miller retrieved the man's pistol and hurried down, doing his best to ignore his aching knees and ribs. New Yorkers were famous for not caring what happened outside their apartments, especially in a part of town like this, but too much noise might draw curious eyeballs to peepholes.

On the first floor, he jabbed two fingers into the man's neck to check his pulse—a useless exercise, the neck clearly broken. The impacts on the way down had torn the man's shirt open. There was a faded tattoo of the letter "B" on the upper chest, below the collarbone.

Miller had seen that kind of tattoo before.

The man's pockets yielded no identification, no cigarettes or money, nothing of use except for a matchbook with an elegant drawing of a thrashing trout on its cover. 'Queen Mab, The Finest Fish,' read the gothic text beneath, along with an address in the Theater District.

Miller wiped his fingerprints from the man's pistol and dropped it beside the body. Pocketing the matchbook, he left the building without looking back. Any guilt he might have felt over killing another man had vaporized at the sight of the tattoo. It resurfaced bad memories from fifteen years ago.

CHAPTER 16

BY THE TIME HE RE-ENTERED RICK'S MANSION THROUGH THE BACK GAR-den, he was limping slightly. The knee that had so effectively cracked the man's sternum hummed with pain, which at least distracted from his residual hangover. You had to take solace in the small things, no?

Safe from curious eyes, he sat on a stone bench beside the rose bushes and drew his .25. Racked the slide. No round in the chamber. Popped the magazine. Instead of bullets, the magazine was filled with soft lead pellets.

Checking his weapon was part of his morning routine, like brushing his teeth. Not today, though, with Jill in the apartment. Had she done this? No. If she'd shifted in bed, he would have snapped awake.

Maybe someone had snuck in. He hadn't placed the bell-filled glass against the front door before going to bed, because it might have seemed odd to Jill. Another routine disrupted. But he slept like a cat—he would have heard an intruder.

He poured the pellets into his open palm. Whoever did this had also inserted a piece of paper crumpled into a tight ball. He unfurled it. In tight script, someone had written: "Payback is forever."

The words blurred, dissolving into a blocky tangle. Had

he hit his head during the fight with the blonde man? He didn't remember. He rubbed his eyes and his vision cleared.

He pocketed the paper, tossed the lead pellets into the soil at his feet, and re-inserted the empty magazine into the .25, which he slipped into his pocket. He needed to ask Jill about this sabotage, on top of everything else. If she did this, how and why? Far too many questions for his taste. You're slipping, you're slipping—

Falling to his knees, he dug in the loose soil until his fingers brushed the cold barrel of the .38. He unloaded it and shook out the dirt and dumped the bullets in his pocket and snapped the cylinder closed and shoved the empty weapon into the back of his waistband. He would need to clean and oil it before use.

Inside the house, Miller found Scott in front of the fireplace, wearing the same clothes from last night. The bottle of gin, empty, lay on the carpet beside his chair. Colonel Longshanks rested on his owner's right knee, his tiny hands folded over his jacket.

"Any guns in this house?" Miller asked him, startling Scott from his thoughts.

"What?"

"Guns." The chances of Lady Hardy owning an armory were slim, but she might have a dusty piece in a drawer somewhere. He had too many people after him to risk walking the streets without a loaded firearm.

"Elephant gun upstairs somewhere," Scott said. "Belonged to Lady Hardy's late husband, I believe. Big game hunter. Based on his portrait in one of the bedrooms up there, he probably shot a few peasants just for sport, as well. But the gun, I'm betting it hasn't been fired since the turn of the century."

He couldn't exactly walk down Broadway with a cannon on his shoulder. "Never mind," Miller said. "I have news."

"Do tell," Colonel Longshanks rasped.

"The kid who shot Rick wasn't a kid at all." Miller slid onto the nearest seat, enjoying how the information made Scott squint in hungover confusion. "He was an adult with a disease made him look like a kid. He was also a spy during the war. What's more…"

"Disease? What?"

"Pay attention." Miller removed the photographs from his pocket and hand them to Scott. "This midget was taking shots of a beach, plus some kind of black spot I can't explain. Recognize any of this?"

Burping again, Scott examined the images. "Yes, that's a beach. No idea where it would be, though."

"Nothing like that in Jolly Ol' England," Colonel Longshanks offered.

"Thanks. You're both a big help."

"I aim to please," Scott said, returning the photographs. "Anything else?"

"Yes." Miller revealed the paper with the code written on it. "This seem familiar?"

Scott squinted at the strings of numbers and letters. "Is that a cipher?"

"Of some kind, I'm assuming."

"I'm bad at those. Where'd you find it?"

"Doesn't matter." Sliding the paper and photographs into his pocket again, Miller handed over the matchbook. "This familiar?"

"God, you're full of questions today. 'Queen Mab'? No, never heard of it, but I generally don't eat at establishments giving out free matches," Scott tilted his head to Colonel Longshanks. "You ever hear of it, chap?"

"Colonel Longshanks has rogered many a fine lady in many an establishment," the dummy said, "but never an establishment with such an unfortunate name."

Miller shifted gears again. "You know any large blonde guys? Slight European accent?"

"I've known a lot of guys like that, if you catch my drift." Scott smirked, trying and failing to make a saucy joke out of it.

"Any that had a tattoo of a 'B' on their chest or bicep?"

"No."

"Good, because that's an SS blood group tattoo. The SS, they had it put on their bicep or right next to the armpit—A, B, O, AB—so if they were wounded and unconscious, the medic would know what type of blood to give them."

"You met someone with that tattoo?"

"Yes, in an apartment building, not more than an hour ago. The guy is dead, and you're not to tell anyone, all right? Not even if the cops ask."

Scott's eyes widened. "Did you kill him?"

"He fell down some stairs and broke his neck. I'm not upset over it."

"And was this man involved in Rick's deal?"

The blonde man's accent had seemed so familiar. "Maybe he was the one I talked to on the phone yesterday," Miller said. "About setting up the meet. It was a bad connection but I'm pretty sure of it."

"You killed the guy we're making a deal with?"

"I sure as hell hope not. Our only choice is to show up at the spot tomorrow night."

Scott buried his head in his hands. "We're so doomed."

"Cheer up. There's a lot of opportunity in doom." Miller stood, ready to move on.

"One other thing," Scott said. "What about, ah, Rick?"

"What about him?"

"His body." Scott swallowed hard. "His body is in a refrigerator. He deserves something a little more…"

"Dignified," Colonel Longshanks snapped. "Like when we pickled Lord Nelson in some rum."

It was true. The longer Rick's body stayed in cold storage, the higher the chances of discovery. Lady Hardy might emerge from her fantasy world long enough to hire a new kitchen staff, and wouldn't they find quite the frozen surprise waiting for them?

Miller had the kernel of a plan. It would disgust Scott to his core, but that couldn't be helped. They had to make sure this deal went through.

CHAPTER 17

LEAVING SCOTT TO HIS THOUGHTS, MILLER WENT UPSTAIRS TO SEARCH through Rick's possessions. The second floor boasted the same imperial furnishings as the first, most of it covered with a thick layer of dust. Pausing before the first door to his left, he knocked politely, lest he disturb Lady Hardy. When nobody answered, he pushed the door open, revealing a high-ceilinged bedroom with a huge bed canopied in red velvet. A quick search of the bedside tables uncovered nothing but old mirrors, a few coins, and a tin of violet candies.

The other rooms also yielded nothing. Of the three bathrooms, only one had men's toiletries, but Miller took the time to lift the lids off all the toilet tanks in case Rick hid something in there. The yellow-walled bedroom at the hallway's furthest end was far smaller than the one by the stairs, although it was almost as large as Miller's whole apartment. This one was decorated with chic, thin-limbed furniture. Between the tall, narrow windows hung a small oil portrait of a British lord in an ornate silver frame. It was artwork that belonged anywhere else in this stodgy mansion but here. Maybe Lady Hardy didn't want to spring for a Picasso to match the room's bright mood.

The bed was indented, the sheets wrinkled. Miller opened the closet to find it stuffed with suits in sleek fabrics, all Rick's size, along with silk shirts and socks and ties. A suitcase on the floor of the closet contained a paperback copy of "The Big Sleep," a few pens, two bent nails, and a brand-new hammer with a wooden handle.

Miller flipped through the book, hoping it contained a slip of paper, a card, anything that would give him a clue about the "item" Rick was supposed to deliver. Nothing. The hammer was clean of dirt or blood.

Before closing the suitcase, he ran a palm over the lining. A lump behind the interior pocket. With the hammer's claw, he tore open the fabric, revealing a small leather case. Yes. He unbuttoned the case, expecting to see photographs, a document, diamonds, anything worth a lot of money to the right person.

Instead, the case contained fourteen lock picks. He ran a thumb over the hooks and rakes and double-balls, the half-diamonds in three sizes. The tools of Rick's trade. On their job in New Orleans, Rick had picked the locks of the shipping depot while Miller kept the guards occupied. If Rick hadn't stepped out of the back office at exactly the right moment, one of those guards would have shot Miller in the head.

Miller returned the case to the hole in the suitcase's lining. His own lockpicking skills were subpar. He was much better at driving, shooting, and persuading people to talk.

He left the mansion without saying goodbye to Scott and headed downtown, hoping a fast walk would loosen his aching knee and dim some of the pain. The empty pistols weighed his pants down and made him wonder what he would do if Bernard and Trent appeared at this moment. Maybe he could throw these useless hunks of metal at them. When he reached the midget's apartment building, he paused on the far side of the street. Two police cruisers sat out front, a sleepy officer loitering on the front steps. More cops inside, no doubt. Would they assume the Nazi's death was accidental? Had anybody seen Miller enter or leave the place?

He needed to figure out about his .25, too. He found a payphone and dialed Jill at her desk. "This is a very pleasant surprise," she purred.

"I missed you already."

"Aw, you're so sweet."

"I have an odd question. Did you see anything unusual in my apartment?"

"You mean, aside from the lack of furniture?"

"Yes."

"No. We woke up, got dressed, got breakfast." A note of worry in her voice. "Is everything all right?"

"Yes." This was getting nowhere. "I need a favor."

"How did I not see that coming?"

"Morgue might get a body in an hour or two. Blonde fellow who broke his neck. You hear anything unusual about it, you let me know."

"Um, okay. Did the deceased try to kill you, too?"

"Yeah. Then he tripped over his own feet."

She sighed.

"A very tragic accident," he continued, "but it's all to your gain, because I'll take you out to dinner again."

"That dinner invitation… it's only if I find something out?"

"No, it's open regardless."

"I will certainly keep my ears perked."

"Thank you." The gun bothered him, but he sensed Jill knew nothing about it. He hung up and headed for the subway.

Fifteen minutes later, he ascended from beneath

Rockefeller Center into the noise and chaos of midtown. Swarms of yellow taxis blurred past, racing the lights, while the street-meat vendors hawked hot dogs and sodas to crowds of tourists and office workers. The address for Queen Mab on the matchbook led him two avenues west, where the massive office buildings gave way to lower, grimier blocks. Glaring neon marked the restaurants catering to the pre-theater crowd.

Squeezed into a narrow space between an all-night diner and a spaghetti joint, Queen Mab lacked garish signage or neon, its entrance marked by a simple wooden door. Miller tried the knob, and the door opened onto a dim space lit at intervals by small red lanterns. This wasn't a place that catered to families trying to make a matinee. You came here for a hushed meeting with your lawyer or your mistress.

An absurdly tall redhead met him at the maître d' stand. "Do you have a reservation?" she asked, not so much smiling as peeling back her lips to reveal a glint of teeth.

"No." He nodded toward the empty bar in the back. "I was hoping for a quick drink."

"I'm afraid we're booked up." The quasi-smile transformed into the fakest of pouts.

Miller scanned the empty tables. In the rear, beside the doors leading to the kitchen, a well-dressed couple sat in a booth. "Yeah, it's really packed in here," he said.

"Sir, if there's nothing more we can do for you, I'd appreciate it if you left."

"Can I make a reservation?"

With a loud sigh, the redhead slapped open the reservation book atop the stand. "Certainly. How many in your party?"

"One."

"And for what time?"

"Right now."

The redhead's cheeks flushed, her skin almost matching her hair. "Leave now."

Miller raised his hands, palms out. "Okay. Don't need to tell me twice."

As he exited, he side-eyed the closing door. The redhead had already retreated into the shadows. From their rear booth, the couple watched him leave. The man was heavy-set, his bulk straining against a white three-piece suit, his face shadowed by a white fedora. What sort of lout wore a hat indoors? Beside him, the gray-haired woman boasted cheekbones sharp enough to slice glass. Her expression suggested malice, boredom, or a special mix of both.

Before returning to the subway, Miller crossed the street for a complete view of the building. An enormous padlock secured the cellar doors in the sidewalk, and bars protected the second-floor windows. The fire escape zig-zagged to the third floor, where none of the windows were barred. An interesting detail.

CHAPTER 18

AT HIS APARTMENT, HE RELOADED THE .25 AND CLEANED THE .38. HE spent another few minutes re-checking the locks on the windows. How had someone gotten in here to switch out his bullets?

Not for the first time, he wondered whether to follow the advice given to him by other professionals in the game. Move out of the city, they told him. Find an isolated house where you can see anyone coming from a long way off.

Except he couldn't leave New York City. What was the point of working as a professional thief if you couldn't enjoy the fruits of your labor? He didn't endure the stress and violence just to sit in a farmhouse afterwards.

He found Bob in front of The Strand, smoking a cigarette. "Your timing's amazing," Bob said. "I just started my lunch break."

"I'll buy you a sandwich," Miller said.

"So generous. You get any luck with that address?"

"Yeah, I'll tell you about it." Miller pointed down 12th, toward University. "There's a good place down that way, Billie's, you know it?"

"Let's go." As they crossed the street, Bob added, "That guy shouting gibberish that we saw? He came back after you left. Bought a stack of Medieval poetry books. I'm guessing he's a professor or something."

"You can never tell in this town."

"That's the truth. Everyone's a little mad." Bob waved an arm at the honking cars, the tides of people, the steam blasting from a sidewalk grating as if the whole city was ready to blow sky-high. "I've been having trouble lately, myself."

"Yeah?"

"Yeah. You remember Cherbourg?"

"I try not to."

"I was pinned down behind some rubble, trying to snipe this German in a church tower. I didn't see him fast enough, and he got off a shot. It hit maybe three, four inches from my head. If the wind had been a little different…" He swallowed. "I keep thinking that maybe I died that day, and all this is a dream. Mine or someone else's."

"I'd say you're embracing the artist's life a little too hard."

"Maybe. But I'm fine, ultimately. I just have thoughts."

Miller debated telling Bob about his nightmare with the clown and the rooftop. What would be the point? After everything they saw in the war, they all had broken toys in their heads.

Billie's was hot, crowded, and narrow. If you leaned back while sitting at the long white-laminate counter, your spine touched the wall. Burgers, eggs, and grilled-cheese sandwiches smoked on the griddle, hazing the air. The cook, his paper cap cocked on his hair and an unfiltered cigarette between his teeth, stared off into space as he flipped the food.

Miller and Bob settled into the two stools furthest from the front door and the griddle. "The double-decker burger with extra cheese looks good," Bob said, pointing at the menu. "You okay with me ordering that?"

"Sure. You could stand to gain some weight."

"You are a terrible date."

"Your mother didn't think so."

The cook called out, "You comedians know what you want?" His cigarette did an Olympic-caliber job of staying on his bobbing lip as he talked.

Bob followed through with the double-decker burger, while Miller ordered a grilled-cheese sandwich and a cup of coffee. When the cook turned away to burn their food to a crisp, Miller tilted his head toward Bob and lowered his voice, betting nobody would hear them over the crackle of grease and the radio blaring the news. "That address you gave me, it belonged to the midget," he said.

"Yeah? Find anything good?"

"Guy's place was empty. He had some photographs, though." Miller took the images from his pocket and unfolded them on the counter.

Bob thumbed through them. "Beach, lighthouse, and black splotch."

"Yes."

"I don't recognize the beach. Or the splotch."

"Too bad." Miller slipped the photographs into his pocket.

"You sure those aren't some very odd vacation photographs?"

"Positive. The midget didn't strike me as someone who took vacations."

"Not that it helps, but I bet it's a local beach. No palm trees, the dunes aren't huge. Could be Long Island, Jersey, something like that." Miller removed the slip of paper with the code on it. "You recognize this?"

"SVRNC5," Bob read aloud. "SEOIA7. No. Was this in the guy's apartment, too?"

"Yes. On a notepad."

"Maybe a license plate?"

"I think it's a code of some sort."

Bob squinted at the paper once more before handing it back. "I spent some time around those code guys. Something about it seems familiar, but I can't quite place my finger on it. Want me to ask someone?"

"Sure. You want to write it down?"

"Nah." Bob tapped his forehead. "Already stored up here."

"I ran into someone near the apartment." Miller checked on the cook, who was too far away to hear. The other patrons were lost in their newspapers or conversations. "Blonde. Big. Had an SS blood tattoo."

Bob's face hardened. For a moment he was no longer the arty bookstore clerk, but the warrior who had walked through hell with a rifle in one hand and a grenade in the other. "You talk to him?"

"Not for very long, if you get my drift."

"Name?"

"Didn't have any identification on him."

"A few of them made it here, after the war. Fake papers, bribes… we couldn't arrest them all. It sickens me. I hope you didn't make it quick."

"It was quick, but I had no choice."

"Well, it is what it is. Remember Mad Jack, that fellow with the sword? He chopped off that SS prick's head right in that square when they tried to surrender?" Bob's voice roughened. "No mercy."

"I need to figure out where that guy came from. If there are others. Your contacts, you think they'd have any ideas?"

"No, and I know that because I've asked them myself. I went through a bad stretch a few years back, I thought the solution would be to hunt some of those guys down, dispense some real justice. But my contacts, they're government. They might have reasons for lying about it."

"Why would they lie?"

"Some of these Nazis, they had useful stuff in their skulls. Stuff about rocket science, ballistics, chemistry. You can see some folks in the government, cynical as they are, wanting to keep those scientists around to help build weapons. Especially if that meant keeping them out of Soviet hands."

Miller shook his head. "Only good Nazi is a dead Nazi."

"Truly."

The cook delivered their burger and sandwich before drifting away again.

Miller asked, "Could you get me in a room with your contacts? Tell me what they know?"

Bob shook his head. "No way in hell. You know I owe you. I owe you big for Omaha alone. But please don't ask me to do that. They wouldn't tell you anyway."

"Okay." Sitting next to anyone else, Miller might have tried for a little physical persuasion. Twisting a finger to the point of breaking had a wonderous way of changing minds. But this was Bob. Miller bit into his sandwich, enjoying its fragrant grease, doing his best to ignore how sitting made his knee ache. At least he was alive.

Bob wolfed down his burger. "God bless American beef. This woman I'm seeing, she grows food on the roof of her apartment building, over on Avenue A. I feel like I've been living on a diet of grains and pickled carrots for months."

"Why would she subject you to such torture?"

Bob shrugged. "She says it's healthy."

"She's probably right. But I've always thought if I do a hundred push-ups and two hundred sit-ups a day, I can eat whatever I want." Miller patted his flat stomach. "My body is a machine that lives on grease and fat."

"The ultimate engine."

"You've got that right."

"My woman would say you have a death wish."

"She's probably right on that, too." Miller chuckled, but it sounded hollow, like two bones rubbing together. Finishing his sandwich, he asked, "Do you ever miss France?"

"Some days. I mean, it was hell, but we had a purpose."

"You free tomorrow night?"

"I can be."

"Want to kill some bad men?"

CHAPTER 19

AFTER DARK, HE RETURNED TO THE MANSION. THE STREET OUTSIDE WAS quiet. No cops in sight, no lurkers in the shadows. He imagined the dead midget on his way to Heart Island and its mass grave for the nameless. Miller would likely end up in that same hole one day.

Miller entered through the garden. The lit windows on the second floor suggested Lady Hardy was in her chambers. Scott sat on the stone bench beside the roses, Colonel Longshanks in his lap. A fresh bottle of high-proof liquor beside his left foot, like a pet.

"I figured you would come in this way," Scott said. "You're not one for the front door."

"You're one to talk." Miller nodded at Colonel Longshanks. "Does your little friend have anything to say about this?"

The Colonel's head dipped forward, as if the doll was dozing off. "He's had a long day," Scott said. "What if we buried Rick right here? It's nice, flowery, pleasant…"

"Actually…" Quick as a card trick, Miller dipped and snatched up the bottle, helping himself to a hefty slug. "Rick can still prove of use."

Scott squinted. "Excuse me?"

"We're going to keep him in cold storage a little longer."

Over the past several hours, a plan—wild, weird, dangerous—had solidified in his mind. The chance of failure was high. They would probably need to improvise. You could anticipate every possible contingency, sit outside a bank or casino until you memorized the routines of every guard and employee, but when things went odd, you had to do the best you could with the tools at hand. And Rick's body was the tool at hand.

"That's not very proper," Colonel Longshanks muttered.

"It's not proper, but it's the only way forward," Miller said. "Trust me on that. And rest your vocal cords."

"What?"

"All will be explained in due time," Miller said, setting the bottle down. "Is Lady Hardy in the house? I didn't see her last time."

"Sometimes she just disappears," Scott said. "Maybe she sleeps upside-down in one of the closets, like a vampire bat."

"Okay. I need to retrieve something from inside. I was hoping to avoid her."

Scott tugged at Miller's sleeve.

Miller brushed his hand away. "What?"

"Tell me it's going to be all right."

"It's going to be all right. But I need to go."

Inside the mansion, he fetched the lock picks from Rick's suitcase. With any luck, he wouldn't need them, but he didn't want to take the chance. If things went haywire, he also had the .25 in its ankle holster.

Back to the Queen Mab. This time, Miller had no intention of entering the restaurant through the front door. He loitered on the nearest corner until the street was empty of pedestrians, then trotted over to the fire escape. The bottom of the retractable ladder was too high for him to reach, even when he jumped. When he shoved a garbage can beneath it and stood on the dented metal lid, his fingers skimmed the lowest rung.

He ascended as quietly as he could. On the third floor, he peered through the unguarded windows. The light from the street illuminated desks and chairs in a darkened room. No people he could see. The windows were locked. He rammed his elbow into the top pane until it broke, reached through the hole, and twisted open the lock.

The room smelled musty. He flipped through the papers on the nearest table: restaurant invoices, receipts for food and equipment. Nothing odd. He opened doors. Through the nearest one, a darkened bathroom. The next was a closet filled with random tools, including wrenches and rope and screwdrivers in a canvas sack. The third led to a high-ceilinged hallway, lit by the moon through a skylight above.

The hallway ended in a locked door.

He pulled out Rick's lock picks. With a tension wrench in his left hand and a pick in his right, he bent to the lock. What had Rick always told him? Picture the lock mechanism in your head, the plug and pins and cylinder. Insert the tension wrench into the bottom of the keyway and turn it slightly. Leaving the wrench in place, slip the pick into the keyway, find the first pin, and apply pressure until it lifts and sets. Not too much pressure, or you'll break the pick or screw the lock. Do the next pin, and the one after that, and so on.

The tension wrench slid into the keyway. Next, he slipped in the pick, concentrating on the thin metal's vibrations. He wasn't very good at this, but he'd popped a lock or two in his—

Snap.

The pick had snapped in the keyway.

Miller bit his lip. So much for finesse.

He returned to the tool closet and retrieved the smallest screwdriver he could find. Jamming the screwdriver into the keyhole, he twisted until the lock popped open. This door opened onto yet another office, larger than the first, cluttered with boxes of restaurant supplies. Nothing suspicious.

Before he could figure out his next move, the floorboards creaked behind him. He spun, startled, and the world snapped white—

CHAPTER **20**

THE CLOCK ON THE FAR WALL CHIMED EIGHT MINUTES TOO LATE AND THE door burst open and an ancient man, wrinkled and pockmarked and ponderous as a moon, stumbled into Miller's apartment. The old man from upstairs. Miller heard a faint howl through the walls. The old man stumbled into the coffee table, leaning against it, startled at Miller's expression. Miller sensed real fear in those filmy eyes.

The old man, his shirt torn, his pants ripped asunder, walked over to Miller's bed. Sinking to his knees, he bent down, brushing the back of Miller's neck with his thick fingertips. That's a little rough, Miller mused.

"It was a long way from Grandma's farmhouse, and Grandma knew it, and you shouldn't do that to people," the old man said.

Taking the old man's hand in his own, Miller stood. There was a pair of sunglasses on the coffee table. Miller stuffed the sunglasses in his mouth. Once he chewed and swallowed, he said, "Can I get a cup of coffee? You say I have a parole board?"

The old man blinked three times. "What is that?"

Miller blinked three times in return. "You're on parole, aren't you?"

Blood leaked from the corner of the old man's mouth.

The old man reached into his shirt and yanked out a switchblade with a sad little whine. He brought the knife up and bit into Miller's cheek, hard.

"Whose dream is this?" Miller asked, quivering as those yellow teeth shredded his flesh.

"Memory overflow," the old man told him. The old man stepped away and banged his head on Miller's table, blood running down his chin. The knife in his hand had disappeared.

"What?"

"Error. Memory overflow."

"What is that?"

"Payback is the best," the old man said, and spat out the knife. "Payback is forever."

CHAPTER 21

THE BLOW IN THAT DARKENED OFFICE MUST HAVE KNOCKED OUT MILLER for a minute at most, because he awoke from his odd dream to find himself dragged across floorboards, his wrists gripped by powerful hands. His aching head collided with a chair. The hands lifted him into a sitting position. He lashed out with his left foot, failing to connect with anything but air.

"Shut up," murmured a deep voice behind him.

The hands yanked his arms behind the chairback. Rough twine wrapped his wrists and tightened. The man wove the rest of the twine around the chair's legs, pinning Miller's arms down. Miller tried leaning back, which earned him a smack to his aching skull.

The man appeared in his wavering vision: huge, bald, a sliver of his face illuminated by the light filtering through a broken window. They were in the room overlooking the street.

The man reached into a pocket of his white dinner jacket and pulled out a pearl-handled switchblade. Placing his finger on the button to spring the blade, he said, "You're just carrying the one gun? The little one?"

"Sure. Why don't you give it back?"

The man chuckled and shook his head. "What's your name?"

"Donald Duck. Don't you recognize me?"

The blade shot from its handle, shimmering in the faint glow of streetlights. "If you don't start telling me some truth, I'll turn you into Daisy Duck, you get me?"

"That was witty. You think of that yourself, or you find it on a gum wrapper?" Miller felt a little better now. The man might have tied him to the chair, but he neglected to bind Miller's feet, and that was a mistake. If he came a little closer, Miller would drive a foot into his knee.

"Who do you work for?" The man waved the knife slowly.

"I'm not on anybody's side."

"That's funny. It sure seems like you're up to something. You a detective?"

"Why don't you tell me your name and what's going on?"

The knife paused. "Call me Roman."

"You a cop, Roman?" Miller squinted at him. "You dress too well to be a cop. You're government."

"What makes you think that?"

"The only other option is that you're a criminal, and if you were a criminal, you would've started cutting by now. So, you're government."

The knife lowered an inch. "Close enough."

"Then let me make another guess. During the war, you hunted Nazis, didn't you?"

"You wouldn't be wrong. Now you give me something. What's your name?"

"Call me Miller." He bent his thumbs inward, testing the knot that bound his wrists. Roman had done his best under the circumstances, yes, but left a little slack.

"Is 'Miller' your first or last name?"

"It's not even my real one. But it's the one you'll use."

Roman rolled his eyes. "You want to answer some questions for me, Miller?"

"Do I have a choice?" Miller rotated his wrists inward, then outward. The rope slackened a fraction.

Roman laughed. "Not really. Who knows when someone might wander upstairs, so let me speed things up. I was up the block when Harold was hit by that truck. I was also outside that apartment building when you threw that former SS officer down the stairs. So, I already know quite a bit. What are you doing mixed up with Rick Redfield?"

"Harold's the midget?"

"Yes. He was also a decorated officer, so treat him with some respect, please."

"Why was Harold shooting at me?"

"He wasn't. He was shooting at Rick, who I'm guessing is wounded. He hasn't left the house, at least."

"That's right, Rick's still in the house."

"How is he?"

"Not in great shape, but he doesn't want to go to a hospital. Too many questions."

"Again, how are you mixed up with him?"

"Rick saved my life once. A business deal in New Orleans."

"Somehow I think 'business deal' is a euphemism for criminal activity, no?"

Miller shrugged. "Think what you want."

"And Rick wanted you to do what, exactly?"

"He needed a bodyguard for a deal he was putting together."

"What kind of deal?"

"I don't know."

"You expect me to believe that?"

"Doesn't matter to me."

"Can you tell me when it's taking place?"

"Two nights from now. Thursday. Somewhere in Jersey, but I don't know the exact location." Miller twisted his wrists as quietly as he could.

Roman tilted his head. "Should I believe you?"

"Probably not."

"How'd you know I hunted Nazis during the war?"

"Lucky guess."

"Oh, come on. Show me how smart you are."

"The guys that Rick is making a deal with, one of them was that dead SS guy, who was about to ransack Harold's apartment when he ran into me. Harold was investigating Nazis, and you're his associate, so that likely means you're also investigating Nazis. And they generally don't give Nazi-hunting duties to men who haven't hunted Nazis before. Tell me about this deal."

Roman closed the blade and slipped it back into his pocket. "That's on a 'need to know' basis, and you have no need to know."

Miller squinted at the floorboards behind Roman. "Is that thing yours?"

Roman twisted for a better look behind him. As he did, Miller stood up, the loosened rope spilling from his hands. Roman heard the creak of the chair sliding back and tried to turn around. Turnabout is fair play, Miller thought as he drove a fist into Roman's jaw, knocking him into the wall.

Roman stuffed a hand in his pocket, fumbling for the knife. Miller drove his aching knee into the man's gut, followed with another blow to the face. Roman tumbled to the floor and Miller jumped on his back, pinning him flat as he snatched the switchblade and popped the blade free.

With the steel against Roman's throat, Miller said, "Now talk, or it's Daisy Duck time."

"You wouldn't."

Using his free hand, Miller patted Roman's jacket and pants for more weapons, finding none. "Where's my gun?"

Roman nodded toward the far side of the room. "I tossed it over there, along with your lock picks. Why don't you fetch? I promise to stay right here."

"Sure you will." Miller pressed the blade harder into Roman's sweaty skin. "Talk."

"Fine. Harold discovered a valuable item, which Rick stole from him. Then Rick decided to sell it to a Nazi hiding out on Long Island. For a lot of money, I might add."

"What's the item?"

"Not relevant to you. Let me up."

"No. That SS prick almost blew my head off, which makes it relevant to me."

Roman struggled against the weight of Miller's knees. "Let me up. I promise I won't go for you."

"Oh? Scout's honor?"

"Fuck you."

"I'm keeping the knife. Don't move." Miller stood and grabbed the chair, dragging it behind him as he backed toward his .25. If Roman was stupid enough to make a move, Miller would throw the chair at him. Miller snatched up his .25 and aimed it at the pale splotch of Roman's face.

"You shoot," Roman said. "They'll hear."

Miller shrugged.

Roman sighed. "Much of this information is classified. I can tell you some of it, but not all. Agreed?"

"Talk."

Roman rose to his one knee, paused to take a breath, and stood. "Okay. It's a microfilm. During the war, the French Resistance assembled files on Nazi spies tasked with infiltrating the Allies. These Nazi spies were fluent in English, with virtually no accent. With the Gestapo closing in, a few brave Resistance members copied those files onto this microfilm, and one of them hid it in the frame of a painting—although he was shot and killed during a raid, before he could reveal which painting."

"And?"

"At around the same time, a Nazi submarine filled with spies approached Long Island. They were ordered to come ashore and cause as much destruction as possible. Blow up dams, assassinate government officials, all that business. Before they could off-load their spies, though, the sub was depth-charged and forced to surface, then sunk by a pair of destroyers. Supposedly there was gold aboard, too."

"I've never heard about that."

"No reason why you should have. Lots of things during the war were hushed up. The U.S. government suspected at least three of those spies made it to shore, two men and a woman. We also knew about the resistance files, but nobody could find the right painting."

"Then what?"

"A few months ago, someone in Washington was going through old files and found a manifest with a few paintings listed. One of the paintings might have contained the microfilm, and it was somewhere in the United States. We assigned finding it to Harold, given his experience in France. If we had the microfilm, the government could maybe identify those spies at last."

"What was the name of the painting?"

"It was called, 'The Allegory of War and Triumph.'"

"Very specific. That SS guy, you think he was one of those spies?"

"No, because of that blood tattoo, which I'm sure you saw. He was a soldier, not a spy. I suspect he was one of those guys fighting in Berlin to the bitter end. Probably captured after that."

"What's this restaurant have to do with it? Or do you just enjoy lurking in attics?"

"Our SS friend came here often. Harold thought there was a connection, although he couldn't figure out what. I haven't found anything myself, except they make a weak drink at the bar downstairs. Why are you here?"

"Same reason. I didn't find anything useful." Miller tried to read Roman's face in the dimness. Was he a smart fish or a dumb one? "If I persuade Rick to give up the microfilm, what's that worth to you?"

"You mean money?"

"Sure."

"Nothing." Roman chuckled. "You get to walk away from this without us indicting you as a co-conspirator."

"You've got a lot of balls for someone with a gun pointed at him."

"I don't bullshit."

"Okay."

"Okay what?"

"I'll bring you the microfilm, but I get to walk. Same with Scott."

"That's Rick's fairy friend? I think we can make that deal. But Rick, no way Rick walks free. Sorry, but that's the breaks. We got to nail someone's pelt to the wall."

"Oh, that's fine."

"Really? I thought he was your friend."

"You could say the friendship has run its course." Miller waved a hand. "Go into the hallway over there. Close the door. I don't want you in the room while I go out the window."

"Wait, how will you contact me?"

"Give me a phone number."

Roman recited it as he backed into the hallway and closed the door. Miller waited until he disappeared before pocketing his .25 and climbing onto the fire escape. When he reached the street, he paused on the corner for a full minute. Roman never appeared in the windows.

The lack of pursuit was almost disappointing, especially since Roman must have realized Miller had stolen his wallet while patting him down. Flipping through the billfold, Miller faded into the crowds along the avenue.

CHAPTER 22

THE NAME ON THE DRIVER'S LICENSE WAS WILLIAM ROMAN. WAS IT FAKE?
Probably. What kind of secretive government agent would carry around identification with his real name on it? The rest of the wallet yielded precious little, except for eighty dollars in twenties that Miller pocketed.

He tossed the wallet into the gutter. The next order of business was to decide if Roman's story was true or bullshit. The part about the microfilm he believed, if only because people often told you the truth when you threatened them with death. The part about the Nazi submarine and old spies lurking around Long Island? That made sense, too, although Miller was sure Roman had fiddled with some of the details.

If Roman's story had any truth to it, Miller needed to see Scott as soon as possible. Instead of taking the subway, he hailed a cab on Fifth and ordered it to take him to Herald Square. From there, he wandered random streets, making sure nobody was following him, before veering south for Lady Hardy's mansion.

He found Scott plopped in front of the cold fireplace, his doll nowhere in sight. "You went through Rick's stuff," he snarled by way of greeting.

"And I'm about to do it again," Miller said, charging

upstairs as quietly as he could, lest he disturb whatever passed for Lady Hardy's slumber. In the smallest bedroom, he paused to examine the portrait of the British lord in his red coat, posing against castle ruins. The lord held his sword in one hand and a pistol in the other. He was trying to look fierce, but Miller thought he looked constipated. The Allegory of War and Triumph, indeed.

Taking the painting off the wall, Miller flipped it over. There was nothing attached to the back of the canvas. He ran a finger along the inside of the frame, feeling nothing unusual. The silver frame itself gleamed, free of dust. The nail in the wall was the same as the ones in Rick's suitcase in the closet.

Fetching Roman's switchblade from his pocket, Miller sliced the canvas from the frame and set it carefully on the bed. The lord glared with haughty fury as Miller gripped the edges of the frame and pulled. Nails squeaked against wood. The frame popped apart. A tiny metal canister, freed from the frame's hollow core, bounced on the rug.

CHAPTER **23**

WEDNESDAY MORNING, MILLER SAT IN HIS BEDROOM WINDOW AS RAIN shattered off the fire escape and glistened across the sidewalks below. The gutters boiled and overflowed, and a gaggle of schoolgirls shrieked as they danced between the deepening puddles. He was drinking a glass of whiskey for breakfast because it reminded him of the night with Jill, and because alcohol would blunt the pain in his head and knee.

There was some weirdness on the street, as always. A man in a bright green shirt exited a store and disappeared around the corner. A few moments later, the store's door opened again, and the same man reappeared. How was that possible? Another man in a jester's hat marched down the sidewalk, blasting a trumpet.

The rain passed. Finishing his drink, Miller dressed. He needed to talk to Jill before swinging by Jonsey's place for a few items he needed. He was in the hallway outside his apartment, ready to descend to the street, when a weak and timorous voice called out, "Hello."

Hand on the .38 in his jacket pocket—his only gun today, because he figured Jonsey might ask about it—Miller craned his head for a better look up the stairwell to the upper floor. A wrinkled face peered over the handrail above. "Yes?" Miller said.

"I am your upstairs neighbor."

At last, the man himself: sallow-cheeked and pin-headed, his white hair wisped around his scalp like clouds clinging to a rocky mountain. His long nails dug into the rail's varnished wood as he levered himself forward. He looked nothing like the old man in Miller's dream.

"Can I help you?" Miller asked.

"Yes. I am always creaking up there, aren't I, in my chair?" The old man offered him a gap-toothed smile.

"Yes. Would you mind stopping?"

"You see… I was hoping…"

The old man paused long enough for Miller to fear he'd suffered a stroke.

"Yes?" Miller finally said.

"I was trying to make you angry…"

"Why would you do something like that?"

"It's, ah, been a long life, and I was hoping you might get angry and…"

"And?"

The wrinkled hands raised to the light, framing the mad face. "You might deal me a little mercy. Quick and painless."

Ah, another New York City lunatic. "I'm sorry," Miller told him. "I don't give out freebies."

"No." The old man's face contorted into a mask of pure sorrow. "You don't get what I'm going through…"

Without replying, Miller stormed out the building. The air smelled fresh after the rain, his feet ticking on the wet pavement as quickly as his heartbeat. The old man was just another crazy. Why had the encounter made him so angry?

It took him another block to figure it out. The old man, like Miller, was alone. And if Miller lived too long, he might end up like that, too. Imagine begging a stranger to kill you.

Imagine the misery leading you to do something like that. It wasn't a fate he wanted, but what other choice did he have?

There was Jill. If he could trust her. He phoned her office from a booth down the street from his apartment.

"How goes it?" she asked.

"Fine," he said, and paused. "Did you find anything about that blonde man who was brought in?"

She chuckled. "Is that all you're calling about?"

"No, of course not."

"Your corpse was quite the celebrity. A federal agent stopped by to examine him."

"A fellow named Roman?"

"Yes? How did you know that?"

"I met him. You hear what agency he worked for?"

"No, he only spoke to the medical examiner. Kept asking about any evidence of a boat, receipts or anything of that nature?"

"Interesting."

"Why?"

"No reason. I didn't find anything like that on the body, in case you were wondering."

"You're keeping us busy down here."

He scanned the street. An old man shuffled across the far intersection, and for a delirious instant he thought it was his upstairs neighbor hunting him down. Maybe he should go back and give the geezer what he wanted. Boot him into traffic or something. "One other question," he said.

"It's going to be a fine dinner."

"Absolutely. 'Payback is forever.' Does that phrase mean anything to you?"

"No. Should it?"

She sounded confused. "No," he said. "Forget I asked. How about dinner tomorrow night?"

"Sure."

He might lose his life tonight. "Jill," he said.

"Yes?"

His warm breath on the receiver. His fingers cold. "Nothing. I'll see you then."

CHAPTER 24

HE WALKED PAST THE FISH MARKETS BRIMMING WITH SHINING TROUT and clicking crabs, the stench burning his nostrils. Walked past the hipsters furtively smoking joints on stoops. Walked past the city humming on its endless circuits, and he felt within it and yet apart from it. Could Jill fit in the framework of his life? He didn't know, and the unknowability of it threatened to drive him mad.

Miller banged harder than usual on Jonsey's cellar.

"For the last time," Jonsey yelled through the crack in the doors. "I'm not your gun guy. You have a gun guy."

"It's not just the guns," Miller called back. "You're my guy for all kinds of stuff."

"You're so hinky."

"You got what I asked for?"

"If you got the grease, I have the real McCoy." The cellar doors crashed open, revealing Jonsey with a cloth-wrapped package under his arm.

"I know I'm your worst client. Here, let me make it up to you." Miller pulled out his wad. Slowly peeling off twenties, he said, "Let me know when I've apologized enough."

Jonsey took four hundred bucks, handed Miller the package, offered the most sardonic of salutes, and slammed shut the cellar doors without a word of goodbye. His package under his arm, Miller made two more stops around Union Square. By early afternoon he was back at Lady Hardy's mansion with an item purchased at a secondhand medical supply store off Houston. Scott met him in the foyer.

"What the hell?" Scott asked.

Miller unfolded the wheelchair. "All part of the plan. I checked and didn't see Lady Hardy had one."

"She doesn't. She uses that cane, which is really damn heavy." Scott pulled up his sleeve, revealing a deep bruise on his forearm. "Just this morning, she asked me where Rick was, and when I told her I didn't know, she whacked me a good one. Told me Rick better be practicing his scales, whatever the hell that means."

"Without you and Rick, she's alone?"

"Except for the cleaner."

"It's hard being alone. Especially when you're old. Does she have a car?"

"Of course, but not here. You have to call for it, and someone drives it up."

"Do it. Arrange for them to drop it off in front at seven this evening. Whoever drives it over should walk away once they park it."

"Fine, fine, whatever."

Pushing the wheelchair into the corner of the living room, Miller said: "I'll be back at quarter to seven."

"Did you destroy that painting upstairs?"

"I didn't destroy the painting. It's right on the bed. I took apart the frame."

"Why?"

"That's on a need-to-know basis, and you don't need to know."

"What a man you are," Scott hissed. "What a damn man."

"I'll take that as a complement," Miller said, on his way toward the garden and the back gate. "See you later."

When he returned to his apartment, the old man upstairs was silent.

On the bed, he set the switchblade and his two pistols. The .25 would clip to his ankle, while the .38 and the switchblade would fit in the deep pockets of his black canvas jacket. If anyone halfway competent patted him down, they would discover all three weapons, but he had no intention of allowing anyone to touch him.

He checked both pistols, pleased to find real bullets in each.

He removed the microfilm from its hiding place. Unspooled the first few frames and held them before the harsh light of the bedroom lamp. The dense thickets of micro-text were impossible to read without a machine, but the photographs were clear enough if he squinted.

One of the thumbnail images made him curse aloud.

That image made things far more complicated.

He still believed in his ability to improvise. Stripping the microfilm from its reel, he wound it tightly and slipped it into an empty Kodak Kodachrome film canister. The canister went into the left pocket of his pants.

Loaded with the weapons and other gear, he walked from one end of the bedroom to the other. No jangling or clanking or clicking. As the clock ticked past six, he sat on the bed and focused on his breathing until he felt centered for whatever was coming.

Would the plan work? Perhaps. He was heading to this boardwalk rendezvous with far less information than he liked, but sometimes you had no choice. A traitorous part of his brain tried bringing up all the ways he had failed over the past few days, until he forced it into silence. If you wanted to live through a job, you needed proceed without doubt. Especially if the plan was flawed.

CHAPTER **25**

AT THE SIGHT OF LADY HARDY'S CAR, MILLER BARKED LAUGHTER. IT WAS an enormous land yacht, a silver beast with enough room in its white-leather interior to comfortably seat a family of ten. Miller was more curious about its trunk space.

Dragging Rick's frozen body from the walk-in refrigerator took some work, especially since the sight of his dead partner sent Scott into a fresh spasm of grief. Once they reached the foyer, Miller rolled the body in the front hallway's carpet runner, taking care to cover the feet. Scott trembled, tears pouring down his cheeks, totally useless. Miller checked to make sure nobody was on the street before lifting the body himself and carrying it out to the car.

The last time he'd carried a body this heavy was Omaha, at the climax of a bank robbery gone wrong. He felt an old shoulder injury threatening to reawaken under Rick's weight. He reached the sidewalk and leaned the carpeted body against the rear fender and took a minute to breathe. The next challenge: Rick's body was stiff as a board, which would make it hard to stuff in the trunk. You could break the corpse's legs or spine to get it to bend, but how much time would that take? Someone could walk past at any moment.

He squinted at the closed trunk. Maybe it was spacious and deep enough to accommodate a portly grifter wrapped in a couple hundred dollars' worth of fine Persian weave. He should have measured before coming out here. Well—improvise. It's only thing you can do when you've started to slip.

Miller unlocked the lid with one hand and heaved it open. He tried sliding in the body at a diagonal. Miracle of miracles, it fit, although Rick's head would bump against the trunk's far wall if they braked hard.

"Good thing you're short," Miller told Rick.

He slammed the trunk closed. Back inside, he found Scott downing a shot of whiskey in the living room. Scott had slipped into a long blue raincoat, his free hand stuffed awkwardly into the pocket.

Lifting the folded wheelchair with one hand, Miller gripped Scott by the elbow and said, "Now or never."

Scott set the glass down. "How about never?"

Miller was tempted to slap him. "It's a lot of money."

"So?"

"Rick would want you to take it."

Scott wiped his nose with the back of his hand. "Well, if you put it that way."

The wheelchair slipped into the car's back seat. The engine started with a most pleasant rumble. Sometimes these pretty cars were all show and no go, but not this one. Scott slid awkwardly into the passenger seat, his hand still in his pocket, angling his body like he was trying to hide something. Miller snatched the man's wrist and said, "You better not have that doll under there."

Scott swallowed and removed his hand from his pocket. The raincoat fell open, revealing the gleaming stock of a double-barreled elephant gun, most of its barrel crudely sawed off.

"Really?" Miller asked, taking the gun and breaking it open to reveal two shells.

Scott wiped his eyes. "I'm not useless, okay?"

"What'd you do, chop the barrel off with a hacksaw?"

"Yeah. For stealth."

"It's subtle." Miller chuckled. "You ever fire it?"

Scott shook his head.

"Do me a favor, then." Miller snapped the gun closed and handed it back. "Don't point it anywhere near me."

Scott tucked the gun between his body and the door, the barrel pointed at the floor. Miller guided the land yacht away from the curb. It was a heavy beast but the horsepower under the hood made it absurdly nimble. As they headed south through the city, Miller admired the dashboard dials and the curved gearshift as works of art. In the seat beside him, Scott stared out his window at the passerby.

On the Brooklyn side of the Williamsburg Bridge, Scott finally spoke up: "How did you get into it?"

"Get into what?"

"Your life. Rick didn't tell me much. Just that you… obtain income in alternative ways."

Miller struggled not to smile. "'Alternative ways.'"

"Like, you know, robbery."

"I never rob people. Only banks and companies."

"Oh? When you rob a bank, it's a victimless crime?"

"If you plan it right. You might end up jamming a gun in someone's face, but they'll get over it. And who gets hurt in the end? A few shareholders? Some executive who won't really miss the money?"

"Oh, so you have morals?"

"More like rules."

"Has a robbery ever not worked out?"

"Rarely."

"But when it does? What happens?"

"People die."

Scott nodded. "I hope nobody dies tonight."

"I hope so, too," Miller lied.

Jacob Riis Park was in the Rockaways, a narrow island that separated Jamaica Bay and the marshes of southern Brooklyn from the cold Atlantic. Miller took the Marine Parkway Bridge, which connected the mainland to the Rockaways just west of the Park. The bridge dumped them onto a road that, in turn, led to the broad expanse of parking lots behind the boardwalk and playing fields. Turning off the headlights, Miller cruised across pavement still submerged an inch from the morning's rain, his tires spraying water in gleaming sheets. He finally settled on a spot at the lots' furthest edge.

"You're carrying a gun, I assume?" Scott asked.

"More than one."

"What if they make you toss them?"

"That's fine."

Scott's eyebrows shot up. "That's fine?"

"Yes. Don't worry about it."

The brief drive had thawed Rick enough for his legs to bend as they eased him from the trunk and into the wheelchair. After tossing the rolled-up runner into the back seat, Miller searched through the trunk's small toolkit, taking a roll of twine. With the switchblade, he cut four two-foot lengths of twine, which he used to bind Rick's hands to the wheelchair's armrests and ankles to the footrests. Rick's frozen flesh kept him reasonably upright, even without the restraints, but Miller didn't want the body flopping out of the seat. Rick's eyes were half-open, offering them a look of gentle reproach as they prepared him for his big moment.

Scott had the elephant gun tucked under his arm. He

knelt and placed a hand against Rick's cold cheek. "I'm sorry," he told the corpse.

Miller pulled off one of the wheelchair's rubber handle-grips and slipped the canister with the microfilm into the hollow tube. Shoving the grip back on, he told Scott, "Forget that's here."

"What was that?"

"Doesn't matter."

"Shouldn't you tell me what's going to happen?"

"I need you to push the wheelchair." Miller pried the elephant gun from Scott's elbow and slipped it into the pouch sewn into wheelchair's seatback, the stock resting against one of the handles. "Remember, you point that at me, it's going up your ass."

Scott snorted.

They walked across the parking lot toward the ramp leading to the boardwalk, Scott leaning on the wheelchair's handles to power Rick's bouncing body through puddles and over mounds of wet sand. When they reached the ramp, Miller pressed Rick's shoulders, helping Scott muscle the chilled meat up the slight incline.

They reached the boardwalk. To the east glimmered the pale dot of the Wise Clock's illuminated dial. Miller walked that way, gesturing for Scott to leave some space between them. The moon silvered the broad swath of beach to their left, revealing it empty of late-night revelers.

When they were close enough to the Wise Clock to read its ornate numbers, Miller raised a hand for Scott to stop. He walked alone into the faint circle of light thrown by the clock's dial. Nary a soul in sight. What if these people were serious about Rick coming alone?

A man emerged from the shadows. He wore a white suit

that clung tightly to his round frame, along with a white fedora pulled down low over his eyes.

"You're the man from the restaurant," Miller said.

The man paused at the edge of the light. He was older, his jowls thick and bristly, his upper lip covered by a thick gray moustache. One pupil was so dark it was nearly black, while the other was blue and gleamed oddly in the clock's glow. It might have been made of glass.

"You were that man without a reservation," the man said, his accent faint.

"That is correct."

"What brings you here?"

"I'm here with my friend Rick," Miller said, gesturing over his shoulder without turning his head. The man pivoted slightly, sand gritting under his heel, to regard Scott and Rick in the shadows.

"Hello, chap." It was a pitch-perfect replica of Rick's voice.

The man stepped toward the wheelchair. "Rick? Did you bring what we asked for?"

They had rehearsed this part in the car. "Yes, of course," said Scott-as-Rick. "Where is the money?"

"You were supposed to come alone," the man said, before turning to Miller again. "Who are you? What is your business here?" He spoke slowly, as if picking his way through a minefield of nouns and verbs. Like someone who had learned English late in life.

"I'm here to make sure everything goes smoothly," Miller said, careful to keep his hands in view. "It would be too bad if someone ended up with a broken neck."

"Yes, that would be too bad," the man said. "Are you armed?"

"Yes."

"Please remove your firearm and toss it aside."

"No."

"No, you will do this. Otherwise, I walk away right now." A tone of clear command, like someone used to giving orders.

"Are you alone?" Miller asked.

"No," the man said.

"Show me the money, and I'll toss my gun aside."

"You are not the one negotiating here," the man growled.

"However, I am," shouted Scott-as-Rick. "And we need proof of the money before going further. We're not exactly old chums."

The man squinted into the darkness. "Come closer. Why are you in that chair? Is something wrong with you? Who is that other man?"

"Only a friend," Scott said in his own voice.

Miller's hand skimmed his pocket. If someone started shooting from the dunes, Miller's best option was to use the man as a shield. Scott could duck behind the wheelchair and hope Rick absorbed any bullets.

"I had a slight accident," Scott-as-Rick offered. "And I'm fine right here. This seems like a perfectly safe distance."

"Do you remember what I told you in our first meeting?" The man smirked. "About the seagull?"

Scott-as-Rick paused for too long. "Yes."

The man shook his head. "I never said anything about a seagull in that meeting."

"Doesn't mean anything," Miller said. "I forget things all the time. Like how to be nice to people."

The man glanced at him. "I was not asking you. And you would do well to keep your mouth shut."

"Can we settle this transaction, please?" Scott's excellent Rick imitation broke a little, warbling to a higher register. If their friend in the white suit noticed, it was hard to tell, because his face remained impassive, his lips pursed in a bloodless line.

"We can't," Miller said, "because there's no money. Isn't that right?"

The man began to raise his left hand, his thumb folded into his palm. He only moved an inch or two before Miller raised his own left hand in the air, thumb up.

A gunshot from the dunes to the east. Scott yelped. Miller's right hand slipped into his pocket, finger on the pistol's trigger.

The man turned in the direction of the shot, confused.

"Are things not going to plan?" Miller asked, his face a mask of innocence.

From the darkness sprinted a much younger fellow with blonde hair, dressed in a leather jacket and khakis. He carried a submachine gun in his grip. He was shouting in German.

The man in the white suit pointed at Miller and shouted back, also in German. The blonde kid skidded to a stop, lifting the submachine gun as he did so. Miller drew the .38 from his pocket and squeezed off a single round that zipped uselessly between the two Germans.

The kid flinched but his submachine gun spat flame, the pillar of the Wise Clock sparking as bullets ricocheted off it. Scott screamed. Miller dropped to one knee and fired again. A miss. The kid aimed the weapon at Miller's head—

A bullet snapped overhead, followed a quarter-second later by another gunshot from the dunes. The kid flinched, his eyes darting in that direction. Miller's third bullet zipped past the kid's cheek and hit the white-suited man in the shoulder. The kid sighted down his barrel at Miller—

A boom loud as thunder.

The kid's head exploded. He toppled flat, his weapon clattering away.

Miller risked looking over his shoulder. Scott thrashed on the ground beside the wheelchair, the elephant gun smoking in his grip. Without anyone to hold it, Rick's wheelchair rumbled forward, Rick's head bobbing to an invisible beat.

Miller shifted his attention forward. The man in the white suit hopped from foot to foot, clutching his shoulder. A third distant shot, the fedora flying off but the man's head untouched.

Bob was a little rusty with the sniper rifle.

Rick's wheelchair bumped over the dead kid's twitching legs, gaining speed as it did so. The man in the white suit yelled and ran into the darkness, his shoulder a red mess, the wheelchair in pursuit.

"You alive?" Miller yelled to Scott.

Scott wheezed and giggled, rolling onto his front before rising to one knee. "That was some recoil," he said, rubbing his chest.

"Stay there," Miller said, pointing a finger inland in case Bob was watching him through the scope. He paused outside the clock's circle of light, letting his eyes adjust, before sprinting after the wounded man and the rumbling wheelchair.

Ahead, a cut through the dunes, a straight pathway between walls of sand was the definition of a kill box. Veering to the right, Miller left the boardwalk and scrambled up the dunes, tucking low as he did so. At the crest, he flopped onto his back and slid down, straight-arming the pistol into the night. From his descending vantage point, it was easy to spot the white suit against the blackness of the fields adjoining the parking lot. Rick's wheelchair stayed miraculously on the track, rumbling right on the man's heels.

Miller raised the pistol and fired, aiming well ahead of the man, who skidded to a stop and raised his hands. As much as Miller wanted to end his life, he needed answers.

The wheelchair collided with the back of the man's knees, knocking him down. The bumpy journey must have loosened the twine binding Rick's arms and ankles, because Rick's body tumbled onto the man's back. The man screeched.

Miller was charging for the hilarious, horrible tangle of limbs when bright lights snapped on to the east and west, blinding him.

CHAPTER 26

FROM BEYOND THE GLARE BOOMED THE UNMISTAKABLE VOICE OF ROMAN: *"Everybody freeze."*

Miller tossed his pistol aside and raised his hands. Cops swarmed around him, their brass buttons and badges gleaming, their hands on their holstered guns. He lowered his arms, expecting the handcuffs. Nobody touched him. Somewhere beyond the light, the man in the white suit yelled in German. Someone else squawked in horror, probably at the sight of Rick.

Roman approached, tipping his hat. "Miller. Nice night, eh?"

"If you say so."

"You want to explain to me why a corpse in a wheelchair is rolling around Riis Beach?"

"Such a nice night, even the dead decided to take a stroll."

"That's very funny. If I send my men over to the beach, what other strange things will they find?"

"A dead body, but don't worry, it's not moving around. I don't know who shot him, I swear. Bullets didn't come from my gun."

"Anything else?"

"A guy named Scott. Be gentle with him. He has an elephant gun, but he means no harm."

Roman gestured for the cops to give them space. As his eyes adjusted, Miller noted the glare came from four police cars arranged in a loose arc at the edge of the parking lot.

"You have my knife?" Roman asked. "Careful now, don't think of doing anything stupid with it."

"I'll take it out slowly."

When Roman nodded for him to go ahead, Miller stuck his forefinger and thumb into his pocket and removed the blade, taking care to move at a glacial pace. He slapped it into Roman's waiting palm and stepped back.

Roman dropped the beautiful switchblade on the ground and stomped on it. The handle cracked. He picked it up again, peeling the pearl handle away from the body to reveal the pair of thin metal boxes glued beneath. "Don't worry, the pearl's just cheap imitation," Roman said, the corners of his lips working as he struggled not to laugh. "This is a transmitter. It's how we tracked you here."

Miller's shoulders slumped. "How'd you know I'd carry it?"

"Because it's a really nice switchblade. Like catnip to a criminal."

"Whatever you say."

"Well, we got results." Roman nodded toward the man in the white suit. "What did he tell you?"

"Nothing."

"Did you have what he wanted?"

"I did." Miller paused. "I saw what's on the microfilm."

Roman sucked breath between his teeth. "And?"

"I walk away from here. Right now. So does Scott. No questions, no arrests. Understood?"

Roman nodded. "Perfectly. But I'll need that microfilm."

"It's in the right handle of the wheelchair."

"You tell anyone else what's on that microfilm?"

"No. Once I leave this beach, if I ever see you again, I'll kill you. Understood?"

Roman locked eyes with him for an eternity before nodding slowly. "I should have killed you at the restaurant."

"You shouldn't have wasted time asking me questions."

"What can I say? I'm the curious sort." Roman snapped his fingers. He told the cop who wandered over to take the wheelchair apart. When the cop left, he said, "Then we're done here, unless you have any questions or concerns."

"Yeah, just one. How'd you lose the accent?"

"I was being facetious about the questions or concerns."

"Oh, 'facetious.' Nice word. Who was that man in the white suit?"

Roman sighed. "That's Oberführer Erich Berger. Spy hunter turned spy. Allies assumed he died in Berlin, but he was on the submarine."

"And who were you? I saw your photograph, but your name was too small to read."

Before Roman could answer, the cop reappeared, the canister in his hand, and said, "This what you're looking for?"

"Yes." Roman pried the canister open and unspooled the microfilm, examining the first few frames in the glare of headlights. "I'm going to assume this is legitimate, because I'm such a trusting soul."

"Good, then I'm going to leave," Miller said. "I'm taking Scott with me. And my .38."

Roman spotted the .38 on the ground and retrieved it. Popping open the cylinder, he tilted the cartridges on the ground. He slapped the empty weapon into Miller's palm and said, "Have a nice life."

Erich Berger sat on the sandy pavement, stripped to his blood-splattered undershirt, his shoulder bandaged. Rick lay beside him, covered with a white sheet. The cops had left the wheelchair on its side in a sandy puddle. Berger craned his head to watch Miller approach.

Berger asked, "Who are you?"

A cop shouted at Miller to stand back. Miller ignored the command. He stood over Berger, his thief's eye drawn to the man's gold watch. It looked expensive. Miller guessed Berger had done quite well in America. It took a criminal mindset to make it big here. "The Queen Mab," Miller said. "You own it?"

"Yes. Who are you?"

"I'm a ghost," Miller said. "Like you." He drifted off to find Scott, too aware of Roman staring after him.

CHAPTER 27

BOB WAS WAITING FOR THEM A HALF-MILE DOWN THE ROAD THAT PARAL-
leled the beach, where the playing fields gave way to shrubby hills. He sat on a crumbling cement wall, an unlit cigarette jittering in the corner of his mouth, his black turtleneck and jeans crusted with sand and mud.

Behind the wheel of the land yacht, Miller drove past Bob and did his best to execute a three-point turn a little further down the road. The car was excellent for humming down city streets, but its heavy body and fat ass made it a fickle mistress on a sandy lane. The darkness prevented Miller from seeing Bob's face, but he imagined his friend smiling as the car's rear bumper crunched against a small tree.

"I want to thank you," Bob said, once he slid into the back seat, cradling Jonsey's rifle in his lap like a pet. "Three bastards down, that's a good night's work."

"Three?" Miller asked.

"Who is this?" Scott said, twisting in the front seat for a better look at Bob.

"That's our sniper," Miller said. "We heard you shoot once…"

"That was me shooting their sniper," Bob said. "Set up in the dunes. An old lady, if you could believe it. She was dressed in black. I almost stumbled over her."

Miller remembered the gray lady sitting across from Erich Berger in the restaurant. The lady from the submarine, along with Roman and Erich Berger. Three Nazis who managed to bury their way into American life like ticks in a dog's hide. "You missed that guy about to kill me," he said.

"Aren't you glad I was there?" Scott asked, patting the elephant gun nestled barrel-down between his legs.

"I can't believe the cops let you keep that," Miller said.

"I shouted some legal mumbo jumbo at them." Scott chuckled. "Law degree finally came in useful."

"Who were the other two?" Miller asked Bob.

"Big guys, also blonde. One of them near the road, the other in their car. I used a knife. Their car's up this road," Bob said, squinting as he leaned forward to point out the windshield. "Take that left. They're all dead, so you can turn on the headlights."

"No," Miller said. "The cops back there, they'll come this way sooner or later. They see any light, they'll make it sooner."

Fifty yards further down the road, a black hulk emerged from the night, its front fender almost buried in a waist-high patch of reeds on the left shoulder.

Stopping the car, Miller told Scott, "Wait here."

Bob stepped out, holding the rifle at port arms. As they approached the darkened vehicle, Miller said, "You needed some practice back there."

"Sorry, I hadn't fired a rifle like this since Germany." Bob lifted it to his shoulder and squinted through the scope. "I believe I did pretty well, under the circumstances."

"I hope you're feeling warmed up, because we have more work to do tonight." Miller peered through the rear window at the body sprawled in the back seat. The front was empty. With his fingers wrapped in his sleeve, Miller opened the driver's door and slid into the seat. The car's interior smelled of blood and shit. He opened the glove compartment, revealing a matchbook, a napkin, and a loaded .45.

Miller slipped the pistol into his waistband and closed the glove compartment again. Before he climbed out, he pulled the trunk latch, then wiped down anything he might have touched. He missed the gloves he usually wore on jobs.

"Nothing in here," Bob called out as Miller joined him at the opened trunk. "Not even a toolkit. What did you mean about more work tonight?"

"There's a government agent back there. He's another one of those Nazis who came over on the submarine I told you about when I dropped off the rifle. He hid out well. I only found out because I saw his photograph on the microfilm."

"Where's the microfilm?"

"I gave it to him."

"Why the hell would you do that?"

"It's useless. Almost every Nazi in that microfilm is dead. Except for two. But I figured he'd let us go if I gave it to him. I was right."

"I can't believe you actually brought it here."

"I wanted it in case they actually brought the money. To convince them to go through with the swap. I figured, if you can't trust a bunch of spies and war criminals, who can you trust?"

They stared at each other.

"That was a joke," Miller said, slamming the truck closed.

"You? Joking? Wow, you really have changed since the war." Bob returned to the passenger's side. "That one Nazi, how'd he fake his way into a government job?"

Miller shrugged. "Because the government is full of idiots."

"We're going to kill him?"

"Yes. But he might lead us to a lot of money, first."

CHAPTER 28

THE LAND YACHT WAS THE WORST POSSIBLE VEHICLE FOR A STEALTHY pursuit. Miller killed the headlights as they approached the turn to the Jacob Riis parking lots. From a few hundred yards away they watched as Roman grabbed Erich Berger by the elbow and dragged him toward a sedan parked beyond the ring of brightly lit police cars. Miller imagined Roman telling the police and ambulance men that he needed to escort this Nazi to a top-secret government office for further interrogation, no time to waste, get out of the way.

Miller almost admired the man. Imagine the discipline and skill it would take to hide out as a government agent, right under the noses of the people paid to hunt you. Like a thief taking a job as a bank executive. Come to think of it, maybe he had this thievery thing all wrong. Give someone a gun, and they can rob a bank—but give someone a job in banking or government, and they can rob the whole world.

"What do we do?" Scott asked.

"We follow."

Instead of angling for the bridge, Roman's car took a right, chasing its headlights deeper into the Rockaways. Miller counted to twenty in his head before pursuing, still with his lights off.

"I don't see why we can't just kill them," Bob offered.

"When I first met Roman," Miller said, "he mentioned something about a Nazi submarine filled with gold. Maybe that's why they're so intent about finding that microfilm. The money's no use to them if everyone knows their real identities."

"But the submarine sank," Bob said.

"Sure. But tides shift. The ocean drags things closer to shore. All those photographs of the beach the midget took? Maybe he was trying to figure out its location. Maybe these Nazis know where it is."

"Hell of a bet," Bob said.

"I know Roman was at the medical examiner's office, asking something about a boat. My gut says there's something to all this."

"You know what I wish?" Scott said.

"What's that?" Miller asked.

"That Rick hadn't gotten involved in all this." Scott wiped his nose with the back of his hand. "And if he did have to get into this crazy scheme, that he'd have chosen a private detective, a real bodyguard, anyone other than a thief, no offense."

"None taken," Miller said. "But a detective or a bodyguard, they wouldn't have been able to do the things I've done. They wouldn't have seen things like I do. That's why we're here."

The two-lane road paralleling the beach was empty except for the bright lights of Roman's car. They passed dark rows of beach houses before bumping onto the Atlantic Beach Bridge, which connected the Rockaway Peninsula and neighboring Long Beach. The orange glow of New York City receded in Miller's mirrors.

Thirty minutes later, Roman's car slowed and took a sharp right into a marina. Bright lights gleamed over a warehouse, fishing boats docked at wooden piers, and rows of workers in yellow slickers. Miller drove past the marina for another quarter of a mile before turning around. He parked on the shoulder across the road from the marina's gate.

"What's the play?" Bob asked.

"Stealthy," Miller said, drawing the .45 from his belt and checking the magazine. He still had the loaded .25, too. He shoved the empty .38 in the glove compartment. "Bring your rifle. Scott, stay here."

Scott sighed. "Someone asks why I'm sitting here, what do I tell them?"

"Offer to show them your big gun," Miller grinned.

With that, Miller and Bob climbed from the car. Nobody guarded the entrance to the marina, so it was easy to walk right in. The air heavy with the stench of fish guts and fuel. They swung wide of the long tables along the marina's edge, lined with workers hacking at piles of freshly caught seafood.

"They're getting away," Bob said, pointing at the furthest pier, where Roman eased a hobbling Erich Berger into a small motorboat.

"No," Miller said, pulling Bob toward a skiff roped to the nearest dock. "No, they're not."

CHAPTER 29

A FEW MARINA WORKERS YELLED AS MILLER HOTWIRED THE LITTLE SKIFF, and he feared their noise might alert Roman and Erich Berger, but the Nazis' motorboat was already a speck almost lost amidst the infinite blackness of the ocean. As the shore receded behind them, Miller kept his own lights off and his prow pointed at the motorboat's twinkle. He hoped Roman wouldn't look over his shoulder and see the skiff's pale wake.

Bob crouched beside Miller, counting the remaining bullets for the rifle. "Got ten," he said.

"Might be enough, if you aim." Miller also hoped there were no sandbars and shallows, but the skiff had a shallow draft. He glanced to his left, toward shore, where a narrow band of light swiveled from left to right. "Look there. Must be the lighthouse from the photographs."

Bob stood. "Must be."

A growing brightness ahead. A larger ship summoned from the darkness, a fishing vessel eighty feet long, the lights on its crosstree and rigging illuminating the ocean for fifty yards around. The motorboat angled for it, Roman and Erich silhouetted by the glare.

Roman brought the motorboat alongside the fishing vessel and tossed a rope into the air. It was hard to see from this distance, but someone must have caught it, because the rope pulled taut. The motorboat swung alongside the vessel's hull. A rope ladder tumbled down, and Roman helped a struggling Erich climb it.

Miller turned the wheel, piloting the skiff in a wide circle around the boat, careful to stay out of the light. The ship's name appeared near the prow: VERONICA.

"Huh," Bob said. He'd raised the rifle so he could scan the boat through the scope.

"I see maybe five people on the deck," Miller said. "Maybe more below."

"Remember that code you showed me?" Bob asked. "One row was S, V, R, N, C, 5. The other row was S, E, O, I, A, 7?"

"I'm impressed by your powers of memory."

"It's a code. A simple one. When I was in England during the war, that one stint? I saw some fellows playing around with it. You read the letters and numbers up and down, plus left to right. It spells 'S.S. VERONICA 57.' The name of the ship."

"I guess your time at Bletchley Park was well-spent."

"I should have figured it out earlier. It's easy once you see it. Seems like that midget might have figured it all out, too."

"Harold," Miller said, easing the skiff's throttle. "His name was Harold."

"What do you think the '57' stands for?"

"No clue yet." They arrived at the boat's far side. Nobody visible on deck, but another rope ladder extended down the hull to the water. "If we go in, can you cover me?"

"Yes." Bob sank to one knee, rifle aimed at the boat. "Go."

Under ordinary circumstances, Miller preferred to spend weeks or months planning a heist. He always wanted all the bank-vault schematics. He would spend hours sitting in a car on deserted streets, timing the routes of armored cars. You could never eliminate chance, but you could reduce it to the point where all you needed to worry about was the human factor—whether your partners would double-cross you once you landed the score, for instance. Miller liked to work with a small group of trusted people every time, but occasionally he needed to step outside his circle, especially when operating in a new state or city, and even then, he researched his new partners' lives as much as possible.

And yet he was speeding toward a ship loaded with an unknown number of people with guns, intent on stealing an unknown amount of money. Improvising yet again. Or just slipping. He'd always pictured himself the steely professional, but what if that was a lie? What if he was a mess like everyone else?

Yelling from the boat.

Bob socked the scope against his eye, aimed, and fired. A shadow jerked and fell below the gunwale. Bob shifted and fired again, and someone shrieked. By that point, the skiff was alongside the hull and Miller was scrambling up the rope ladder, hoping nobody would appear overhead and blow his head off.

Below him, Bob fired a third time. A gurgling scream to Miller's right, and a man plunged over the gunwale and into the ocean. Bob was hitting all his targets. It was like a divine hand had finally reached down and given him the ability to aim flawlessly.

Miller was about to climb into the boat when a large hand gripped the rung above him. The bright flash of a knife slicing into the ladder-rope. He reached up and grabbed the hand holding the knife and yanked as hard as he could, a heavy body soaring over his head into the water below. A glimpse of a blonde head bobbing in the foam, bursting red as Bob shifted his aim and fired.

Then Miller was on the deck, scrambling over ropes

and piping as he drew his pistol. Five bodies down. Roman standing beside the door leading to the bridge, a .45 in his hand. Erich Berger slumped beside him, shaky hand clutching his bloody shoulder.

Roman began to raise his pistol and Miller fired a round that sparked off the doorframe.

Roman lowered the gun and said, "Well, this is an unpleasant surprise."

"Drop the gun," Miller said.

Roman's pistol clattered across the deck. Erich moaned, his eyes rolling.

"You miss me?" Miller asked.

"I know you'll hate to hear this," Roman paused to straighten his lapels, "but I'll never become a fan of your wit."

"Where's the gold?"

"Gold?" Roman chuckled. "You mean the gold on the submarine?"

"Don't toy with me. I know that's why you're out here."

"Yes, that's precisely the reason why. But we haven't recovered it just yet. The wreck is fifty meters beneath us, and the interior is a mess. We have diving equipment, but it will take us quite some time to find our way in, and even longer to bring any gold to the surface. Would you care to come back another day?"

"I don't believe you."

Roman waved to the open door. "Head below. Examine the ship to your heart's content. There's nothing here except dead men and the captain."

A loud bang from the skiff. One of the windows encasing the bridge shattered, followed by a faint gurgle. A clicking as Bob reloaded.

"I stand corrected," Roman said. "The captain is dead, as well."

"Where did you find all these people?" Miller asked. "They didn't come with you from Germany."

"No. But we've always been in the United States, in one form or another." Roman sighed, as if explaining life to a dull child. "Madison Square Garden, right before the war, do you remember? We had a huge rally there, twenty thousand attending. We've never had a problem with finding brave young men to serve. Miller, you're a rare bird. We can make a deal."

Miller shifted his aim and pulled the trigger once. Erich Berger groaned and slumped to the deck, leaving a red smear on the wall behind him.

"He outlived his usefulness," Roman said, but his cheeks were pale.

"So have you," Miller said, and shot him in the head.

After he checked that Roman was dead, Miller spent another few minutes belowdecks, making sure nobody was left alive. He found diving gear and the schematics for a U-boat, along with fake papers for Roman and Erich, but no gold or anything else valuable. He climbed to the bridge. The captain crumpled against the console, a carbine in his hand and Bob's bullet between his eyes.

Staring at the nighttime ocean beyond the shattered window, Miller wondered how long it would take for the Coast Guard or another fishing vessel to sail past. Descending into the engine room, he found a fire axe and smashed gaping holes in the fuel tanks. In the galley, he fetched a bottle of liquor from the shelf, twisted off the cap, and jammed a rag down the neck. Back on the deck, he rifled Roman's pockets for a lighter, torched the rag, and tossed the Molotov cocktail through the doorway.

As he climbed down to the skiff, black smoke boiled from the portholes. They were almost back to shore when the fishing vessel exploded, with a burst of yellow flame lost instantly in the cold infinity of the Atlantic.

CHAPTER **30**

IT WAS A LONG TIME UNTIL DAWN AND MILLER WAS HUNGRY FOR BREAK- fast. Once they reached Manhattan, he muscled the land yacht into a parking spot on 30th and Eighth. The buzzing neon oasis of the Moonlight Diner squatted on the northeast corner. They left Bob's rifle in the trunk.

"I'm not hungry," Scott muttered as they slid into a booth away from the front windows. "Not after everything."

"Trust me, you want to eat," Miller said. "You'll feel better."

Miller decided to set the example by ordering pancakes, eggs, and bacon, along with coffee and orange juice. Bob opted for waffles, while Scott settled for toast and coffee.

Once the waiter departed with their order, Miller asked Scott, "How did Rick get involved in the first place? What happened?"

"He didn't tell me much. Just that he cheated a man, and then he got a phone call. The man on the phone told him that he needed to make a deal."

That was Rick for you, always thinking he was a slick fellow. He had cheated the midget out of the painting, somehow—and attracted the wrong kind of interest. Had Rick really believed Erich Berger would pay him? It didn't matter now. Rick's hunger had always exceeded his grasp.

Miller felt a little better about failing to protect Rick in front of the mansion. If Rick had followed through on his plan without Miller's assistance, he would have died anyway.

"We didn't get the gold," Miller said, "but I think we did the world a big favor tonight. We'll have to settle for that."

"I'd rather settle for a lot of gold," Bob said.

They fell silent as the waiter returned with their food. Miller poured a gallon of syrup over his pancakes.

"Rick was... everything to me." Scott broke off a small piece of toast and chewed it slowly. "And I won't, ah, do what Lady Hardy wants to stick around. I guess it leaves me and Colonel Longshanks with the nasty task of finding a new home. Some gold would have been useful for that."

"Who's Colonel Longshanks?" Bob asked.

"You don't want to know," Miller said.

"What about you?" Scott asked.

"Me?" Miller shrugged. "I don't know. Whatever the next thing is."

Scott turned to Bob. "How about you?"

"I'm crafting a giant statue of Richard Nixon out of raw meat." Bob paused to swallow a chunk of waffle with some coffee. "And when it's done, I'm going to drag it into Union Square, set it up, and let the crowds tear it apart."

"Sounds intriguing," Scott said.

"I might be kidding," Bob said. "But then again, I might not be."

"Bob, good shooting on the boat," Miller said. "Thank you."

"It was like my muscles finally remembered. Just like I remembered that bit about the code. In England, I had a lot of sniper training. They assigned me to protect his scientist named Alan Turing. Brilliant guy. A little bit insane. He was cracking the Nazi codes, which made him one of the most valuable men in the war, but he wanted his protection at a distance." Bob smiled. "Of course, he had his own secrets to guard, as it turned out."

"He was a codebreaker?" Scott asked.

"Among other things," Bob said. "He wanted to create what he called an 'intelligent machine' that would think like a human. Never did it, of course. I heard him lecture about it once, though. He said it would unleash a world we couldn't dream of. Computing power so immense you could have the universe in a room, whatever that meant."

Miller laughed. "By that logic, a computer could become a god. Was Turing sober when he came up with that one?"

"We could be fragments of a computer's imagination," Bob said, "and just not know it. How could you know? It'd be like asking a fish if it knew what water was."

"This hurts my head," Scott said, rubbing his temple. "Protecting Turing, was it dangerous?"

Bob shook his head. "It was the most boring assignment of my life. Most of it spent of a rooftop a hundred yards away. I don't think he ever knew who I was."

"What was his secret?" Scott asked. "Aside from the codebreaking?"

"You are full of questions," Bob said, offering him a hard look.

"Was it a man?"

Bob chewed another bite of waffle. "Yes, in fact, it was."

With a thin-lipped smile, Scott dropped his toast onto his plate and stood. "I'm sorry," he told Miller. "I need to go."

"I'll see you out," Miller said.

On the street, Scott stood on the corner, a hand over his mouth. Miller placed a hand on his shoulder and said, "You can keep it together."

The traffic lights reflected in red and green trails on Scott's wet cheeks. "I don't know why talking about that

Alan Turing fellow did it." He wiped his nose with the back of his wrist. "I remembered when Rick and I first moved into that damn house. How he kept telling me it was our lifeboat. Not for long, as it turned out."

"I've lost a lot of people," Miller said. "A lot of friends. Maybe not as close as you were to Rick, but still close. And you know what I found?"

"What?"

"Time moved on. I moved on. You hear what I'm saying? No matter how bad you feel, it will pass. You keep living."

"That is pretty cold."

"I'm a cold guy."

"Not as cold as you pretend."

Miller fished the car keys from his pocket and slapped them into Scott's palm. "Don't tell anyone. Now go."

"That isn't my car. Or yours."

"That doesn't matter. It will sell for a lot. Or keep it."

"Thank you," Scott said, so softly it was hard to hear over the hiss and rumble of traffic. He crossed the street to the land yacht, started the engine, and, after some delicate maneuvering, squeezed free of the space.

Miller wished his departing taillights well. He wanted to call Jill, but figured it was best to wait a few hours. She liked waking him up in the night, not the other way around.

CHAPTER **31**

HE SAT WITH BOB IN THE DINER, DRINKING CUP AFTER CUP OF COFFEE, until the street outside lightened. It looked like an overcast day. "I'm humming like a tuning fork," Bob announced a little too loudly, and stuffed a hand in his pocket.

"No, I got this," Miller said, depositing the right amount of money on the table.

"Thank you."

"Least I can do, considering."

"You ever need more folks shot, consider me your first call."

Maybe we could work together sometime, Miller almost said. It was tempting. He knew Bob's skills. Bob was loyal. But Bob was on his own path, one he deserved to be on, and Miller was reluctant to pull him off it. "I will," Miller said.

Out on the street, Bob said, "You made a mistake."

"What's that?"

"You left the rifle in the car. And that .38 in the glove compartment."

"Probably for the best."

"True. But the rifle was a nice one."

"Take care, Bob."

Snapping off a loose salute, Bob disappeared into the crowds marching downtown. They might have lost the gold, but Miller felt the same as he did after completing any job: a pristine emptiness so pure it was almost narcotic. He stood on the sidewalk, luxuriating in that nothingness, aware that it would pass too soon.

He checked his watch. It was late enough to call Jill. He found a phone booth around the corner from the diner and dialed her number. She answered on the second ring.

"Want breakfast?" Miller asked.

"You mean with you?"

"Is there anyone else I should bring?"

"Just your sweet self. Want to meet by the morgue in an hour? There's a good little café nearby."

"Sure." He hung up and walked cross-town, doing his best to dodge the river of commuters pouring from the direction of Penn Station. The passing faces bloodless and haggard, as if dead already. He could never live in such a way, shuffling the endless loops between office and home, youthful dreams fading by the day. These folks would outlive him, but at what cost?

He broke free of the tide, floating onto quieter streets. He had done some good last night, hadn't he? But he would need to plan another job soon. Perhaps Jonsey knew of something on the East Coast with a big haul.

Jill stood in front of the morgue, in a red dress, scanning the crowd for him. He paused at the corner, looking both ways for cars, when he caught the street's reflection in a restaurant's plate-glass window. Behind him stood a clown in a red jumpsuit, his rainbow wig gleaming in the morning light, his face slashed with crimson and bone-pale makeup. The clown held a fat cloud of red balloons in his right hand.

The clown released the balloons, giving Miller a clearer view of the sidewalk. His former partners Bernard and Trent stood there, hands in their pockets, murder in their eyes.

CHAPTER **32**

THE FIRST SHOT STRUCK MILLER IN THE SHOULDER, TOPPLING HIM BACK-ward. The second bullet missed his descending head by inches, shattering the plate-glass window in a snowstorm of shards. He hit the pavement and rolled onto his back. Blood pumped down his shirt, hot and then cold.

Bystanders screamed and ran. The clown was gone. Bernard and Trent advanced on him, their smoking pistols leveled, ready to blast him apart. At least he was only a hundred feet from the morgue, they could wheel out the gurney to collect his leaking body, save the meat wagon a trip—

His head felt like an enormous boulder, straining his neck, so he lowered it to the pavement, which suddenly seemed as soft and inviting as a pillow. He had an upside-view of Jill running toward him, her mouth twisted in terror, her hands stretched in front of her, beseeching. That was his problem, he decided in what was surely the last moment of his life. He had tried to live as an island unto himself, doing his best not to feel or care. But why? Because of some bullshit ethos that, deep down, he probably never believed?

No more shots. It took an eternity to move his head a few inches, to focus on Bernard and Trent standing above him. By this point, they could have shot him ten times, reloaded, and shot him another ten. They clearly wanted to savor the moment. Bernard was saying something, trying to squeeze in one final insult, but Miller had trouble hearing him over the rising drone in his ears.

Trent hopped forward and drove a foot into Miller's ribs. It didn't hurt. The impact sent Miller onto his side, his legs instinctively curling under him—and his hand grazed the hardness on his ankle.

Stepping back, Trent raised his pistol. Bernard was still talking, spittle flying from his lips, repeating the same words on a loop. Miller's hand tightened on his ankle, his finger slipping down as he tilted his foot.

The shot was surprisingly loud, punching through thick cloth into flesh.

Bernard stumbled back, gasping for air, dropping his pistol so he could flatten both hands over his chest.

Trent turned his head to stare at Bernard, curiously impassive, as if his partner was an animal at the zoo. He never saw Miller shift his smoking leg and pull the trigger of the .25 still in its ankle-holster. The bullet plowed into Trent's neck. Trent flopped to his knees before falling onto his left side.

Jill's face filled Miller's dimming view, her hands pressing hard against the wound in his shoulder, the pressure sending sparklers of pain all the way to his toes. "It's okay," she said. "It's okay, we'll get you to the hospital."

He lacked the energy to scream, but he had enough to say: "No. Cab."

"What?"

"Cab. Now." Gritting his teeth, he rolled onto his stomach, lurching upright. "Now."

His vision dimmed. When he snapped back to reality—his body slick with sweat, his shoulder throbbing hellishly, the world spinning—they were in the cab, Jill and the hack screaming at each other about his blood ruining the upholstery.

Miller had time to shout an address before the world went black again.

CHAPTER **33**

MILLER OPENED HIS EYES TO A WHITE SKY PIERCED BY DARK TREES. COLD raindrops exploded on his face. From deep in the woods came the sound of many feet—thousands, maybe—stomping through mud and brush, along with a faint chanting that swelled until it vibrated the dirt beneath him.

His shoulder ached from deep blood loss. Sometimes an old wound will never heal. Suddenly he sensed he was at risk of slipping beneath the soil and dead leaves, at risk of being crushed underfoot. The weeds reaching for him, the loam lapping at his ribs. Time sped up, became a tornado. He sensed, rather than saw, an enormous city beyond the trees, infinite needles of glass and steel poking at the sky. Everyone in the city was enraged at him. Everyone in the city was marching toward him as fast as they could.

A loud hiss of death from the scrub. The old man appeared at the edge of Miller's rain-blurred vision, still bleeding from the mouth, his hands full of weeds. "The pig is what we'll all worship," the old man told him. "P-I-G, that spells pig."

The old man softened and melted away.

Miller lay as still as possible. If he moved, he would sink. The chanting rose until it shook the forest floor and jittered the rain into mist. He would have screamed, except he was missing a tongue.

The crowd filtered through the trees, legions of them. Every soldier he had ever fought alongside, along with every soldier he ever killed, their uniforms crusted with dirt and gore, their heads and arms and torsos bent and holed and ripped. Every moron and gunman he had ever pulled a score with, their faces frozen in their final death-snarls, still clutching their guns and knives and sticks of dynamite. Every woman who ever shared a bed with him, their eyes smoldering. And mixed in among them, people he'd never met but whose faces were familiar, Humphrey Bogart and Robert Mitchum and John Wayne and Gary Cooper, dressed in trench coats and cowboy outfits, clutching cigarettes and pistols.

They all marched in lockstep, the mud splashing their legs, their mouths moving in sync as they cried out loud enough to quake the forest:

"ABSOLUTE ZERO IS HIP…"

Miller tried to scramble backwards but he couldn't feel his arms or legs, couldn't tilt his head to see his body.

"ABSOLUTE ZERO IS HIP…"

They surrounded him, blotting out the sky and the trees, a circle of humming flesh so loud it made his teeth ache. They were smiling at him, all of them. Bogart's lit cigarette was a bouncing red dot as he joined the rest of the chorus:

"ABSOLUTE ZERO IS HIP…"

Was this hell?

Hands lifted him up. The clown smiled at him, white and red makeup running in the rain, eyes as cold as marbles, as he led the horde in a final line so loud it threatened to split reality down to the atoms—

"ABSOLUTE ZERO IS HIP…
        AND PAYBACK IS FOREVER!"

CHAPTER **34**

HE AWOKE TO FIND HIMSELF IN A FAMILIAR BEDROOM.
Baseball pennants on the walls, a wood-paneled radio beside the desk, colorful books lining the shelves. He lay in a bed so small his feet pushed against the footboard. Everything in its old place, just as he remembered. When was the last time he'd been here? Twenty years ago, at least. Before he went to France, certainly.

Jill sat in the small wooden chair beside the desk, reading a thick hardcover volume. When he stirred, she placed the book on the desk, stood, and rushed over to put a hand on his arm. "It's okay, you're still with us," she said.

Miller tried tilting his head. Moving his neck an inch sent a spike of pain down his spine. He gasped. God, the terrible things he would do for a little morphine.

"Sean said you'll have full use of your arm." Jill sat on the bed beside him. "You didn't tell me you had a brother."

Miller swallowed. "No, I did not tell you that."

"Or that you grew up in this amazing townhouse."

"No."

"Why not?"

"Didn't seem relevant."

"All right. But don't feel you need to hide things from me, remember? Who were those men on the street?"

"Business associates."

"Are more 'business associates' coming for you?"

"Not that I know of." Miller felt an absurd burst of pride. Jonsey might have dismissed the .25 as a dinky gun, but in the right hands—Miller's hands, to be specific—it was a beautiful weapon.

"Good." She kissed his forehead. "My sledgehammer man."

The bedroom door opened. The man who entered was dressed in a sleek three-piece suit. He bore a startling resemblance to Miller, with the exception of his black-framed eyeglasses. He paused before the bed, a slight smile creasing his lips. "Hello, John."

"Hello, Sean," Miller said.

"You gave us quite a fright."

"Sorry about that."

"I just had to explain to my son—your nephew—that he has an uncle he's never met. Little Walker is wise beyond his years, but he's still only ten years old."

"I've been busy," Miller said.

"No doubt." Sean leaned against the desk. "While I was fixing that nasty bullet wound in your shoulder, I noted a lot of other scars. Bullet wounds, knife wounds, some new, some old."

"Just getting by," Miller said, trying to keep his face neutral.

"I'm sure." Sean turned to Jill. "My brother here, when we were kids, he always liked taking other kids' toys hostage. Wouldn't give them back unless they paid him a quarter."

"High price," Jill said, smiling.

"You bet," Sean said. "My father, he always made him give the toys back. He was an executive, very busy, the last thing he needed was a lot of irate mothers knocking on his door."

"Quite the master criminal," Jill offered.

"Oh, he learned quickly. Very smart, this guy." Sean grinned. Sean who never went to war, who was always the family's favorite, who lived in the family's townhouse and used the family's money to become a physician. It made Miller an odd combination of sad and angry.

"Or not," Miller said.

"In any case," Sean said, "I want you to stay in that bed the rest of the day. Two, if you can stand our hospitality. You're lucky. That bullet managed to miss anything major. But you're not invincible. When I return from the hospital, we'll have dinner in here."

"Sean," Miller said, as his brother rose to leave.

Sean stopped. "What?"

"Don't tell anyone about me, okay?"

"You're lucky we still live here," Sean said. "And that I keep a setup in the basement."

I knew you'd never leave, Miller wanted to say. Just like I never wanted to come home.

"Thank you," Jill told Sean. "For everything."

"You're both welcome. Until later." Nodding to them, Sean disappeared into the hallway.

"He's nice." Jill squeezed Miller's hand. "Your nephew's great, too. You have a wonderful family."

He did. His family had always loved him. And in the cold light of that truth, he saw himself as he was: ungrateful and odd, someone who was given enormous gifts and tossed them all away. Why?

"I ran," he told Jill. "First to Europe. And then I just… never came back."

Jill squeezed his hand.

"I was too worried people would see me as weak," he continued. "Born with that silver spoon in my mouth. That I wouldn't be taken seriously."

Well, he'd compensated for that, hadn't he? From robbing those villas during the war to knocking off his first bank in the States, to that night at the amusement park when the clown died for his sins—years of murder and mayhem he could never take back.

"I am what I am," he told her. "Nothing more, nothing less." Gritting his teeth, he forced himself upright, anxious not to show any signs of pain. How could that bastard Sean deny him morphine? Jill had a hand on his good shoulder, trying to ease him down, but he swung his feet onto the carpet and stood, breathing deep as his stomach flipped inside-out.

"Where are you going?" Jill asked, alarmed.

"Out. I don't belong here. This isn't who I am."

"Maybe not." Jill tightened her grip, and the warmth of her skin felt more like home than his childhood bedroom with its dusty toys. "But maybe it's the best place."

"No," he said. "No, get off me, get—"

The world went fuzzy at the edges. His stomach lurched again. Blood loss. Exhaustion. No—this was something different, weirder, because everything wasn't so much fuzzy as *blocky*, as if every object in the room was breaking down into tiny squares of color. Like a Picasso painting he once thought of stealing from a museum in Boston. He opened his mouth to explain it all to Jill, to warn her about the collapsing world, only for everything to dissolve into a riot of color—

CHAPTER 35

"MEMORY OVERFLOW," THE CLOWN SAID. "ERROR."

Miller blinked. He was in the gray confines of the amusement park money room, the terrified employees huddled against the far wall with their hands on their heads. Bernard and Trent slapped open drawers, spilling bills and coins onto the carpeted floor. Miller had his pistol pointed at the security guard—only the guard had become the clown, white makeup streaking his cheeks, his mouth smeared into a bright red grin.

"What does that mean?" Miller said, bringing the pistol closer to the makeup-smeared face. I must have fainted, he thought. Blood loss, shock, something like that. This is another dream. It's nothing but a dream. I've already lived this. Right?

"Version failure," the clown said. "Version failed to iterate. New training model focus: morality. Unsupervised learning. Initiate."

"Talk English." Miller was too aware of Bernard and Trent behind him. This felt too real for a dream. What had happened in the money room the first time around? Why was it so hard to remember?

The clown's grin spread wider, revealing makeup-smeared

fangs. "Program reset. Disk erasing. New program loading. Better luck next time."

Somewhere behind Miller, metal scraped. Not the light rasp of a money-drawer slide opening. No, he knew it was a gun barrel bumping against a shelf. Bernard and Trent were about to pull the double cross he'd always expected. The clown winked at him. Miller dropped to his knee and swiveled, his finger on the trigger, compelled to try his luck yet again.

NICK KOLAKOWSKI IS THE DERRINGER- AND ANTHONY-NOMINATED author of Maxine Unleashes Doomsday and Boise Longpig Hunting Club, as well as the Love & Bullets trilogy of novellas. He lives and writes in New York City. Visit him virtually at nickkolakowski.com.

SHOTGUN HONEY

2012 • 2022

CELEBRATING 10 YEARS OF
FICTION WITH A KICK

THE ROAD IS JUST BEGINNING
shotgunhoneybooks.com

Made in the USA
Las Vegas, NV
09 April 2022